CHICAGOLAND
DETECTIVE AGENCY

N°1

The Drained Brains Caper

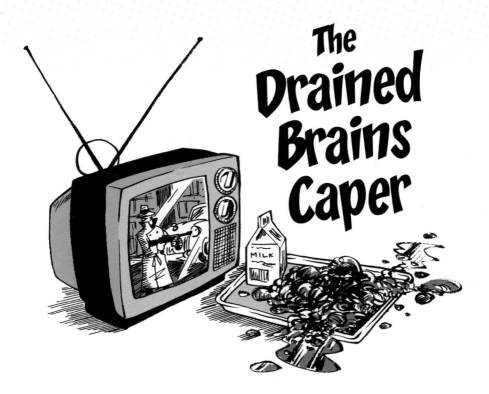

TRINA ROBBINS

ILLUSTRATED BY T!

D1005273

GRAPHIC UNIVERSE™ • MINNEAPOLIS • NEW YORK

STORY BY **TRINA ROBBINS**

PENCILS AND INKS BY **TYLER PAGE**

LETTERING BY **ZACK GIALLONGO**

Copyright © 2010 by Lerner Publishing Group, Inc.

Graphic Universe™ is a trademark of Lerner Publishing Group, Inc.

Graphic Universe™
A division of Lerner Publishing Group, Inc.
241 First Avenue North
Minneapolis, MN 55401 U.S.A.

Website address: www.lernerbooks.com

Library of Congress Cataloging-in-Publication Data

Robbins, Trina.
        The drained brains caper / by Trina Robbins ; illustrated by Tyler Page.
            p.   cm. — (Chicagoland detective agency ; #01)
        Summary: Required to attend summer school after moving to Chicagoland, thirteen-year-old manga-lover Megan Yamamura needs help from twelve-year-old computer genius Raf Hernandez to escape the maniacal principal's mind-control experiment.
        ISBN: 978-0-7613-4601-2 (lib. bdg. : alk. paper)
        1. Graphic novels. [1. Graphic novels. 2. Conformity—Fiction. 3. Schools—Fiction. 4. Computer programs—Fiction. 5. Japanese Americans—Fiction. 6. Latin Americans—Fiction. 7. Science fiction.] I. Page, Tyler, 1976– ill. II. Title.
    PZ7.7.R632Aae 2010
        [Fic]—dc22   2009032620

Manufactured in the United States of America
2 – BC – 12/1/10

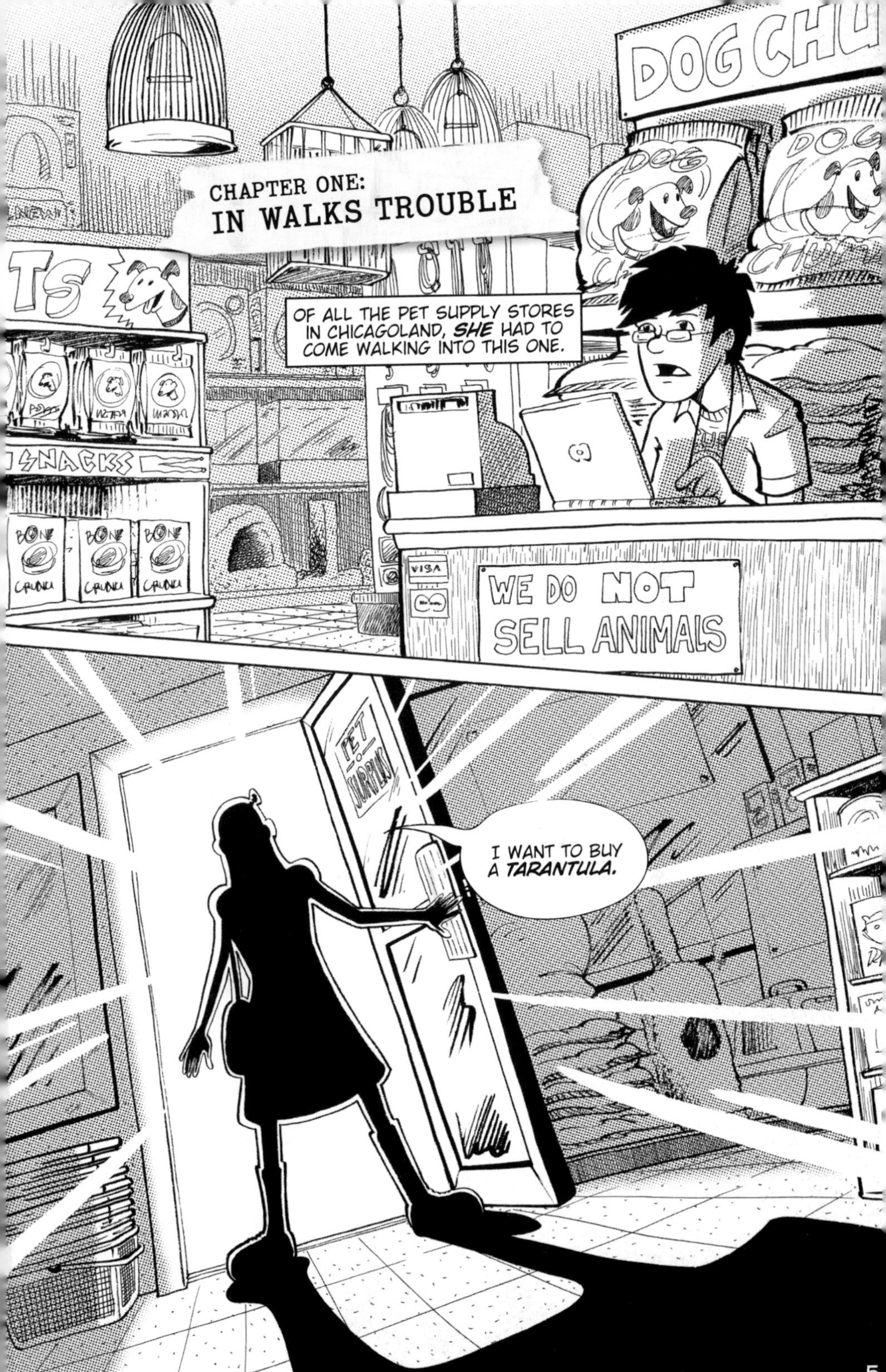
CHAPTER ONE:
IN WALKS TROUBLE
DOG CHU
OF ALL THE PET SUPPLY STORES IN CHICAGOLAND, SHE HAD TO COME WALKING INTO THIS ONE.
SNACKS
VISA
WE DO NOT SELL ANIMALS
I WANT TO BUY A TARANTULA.

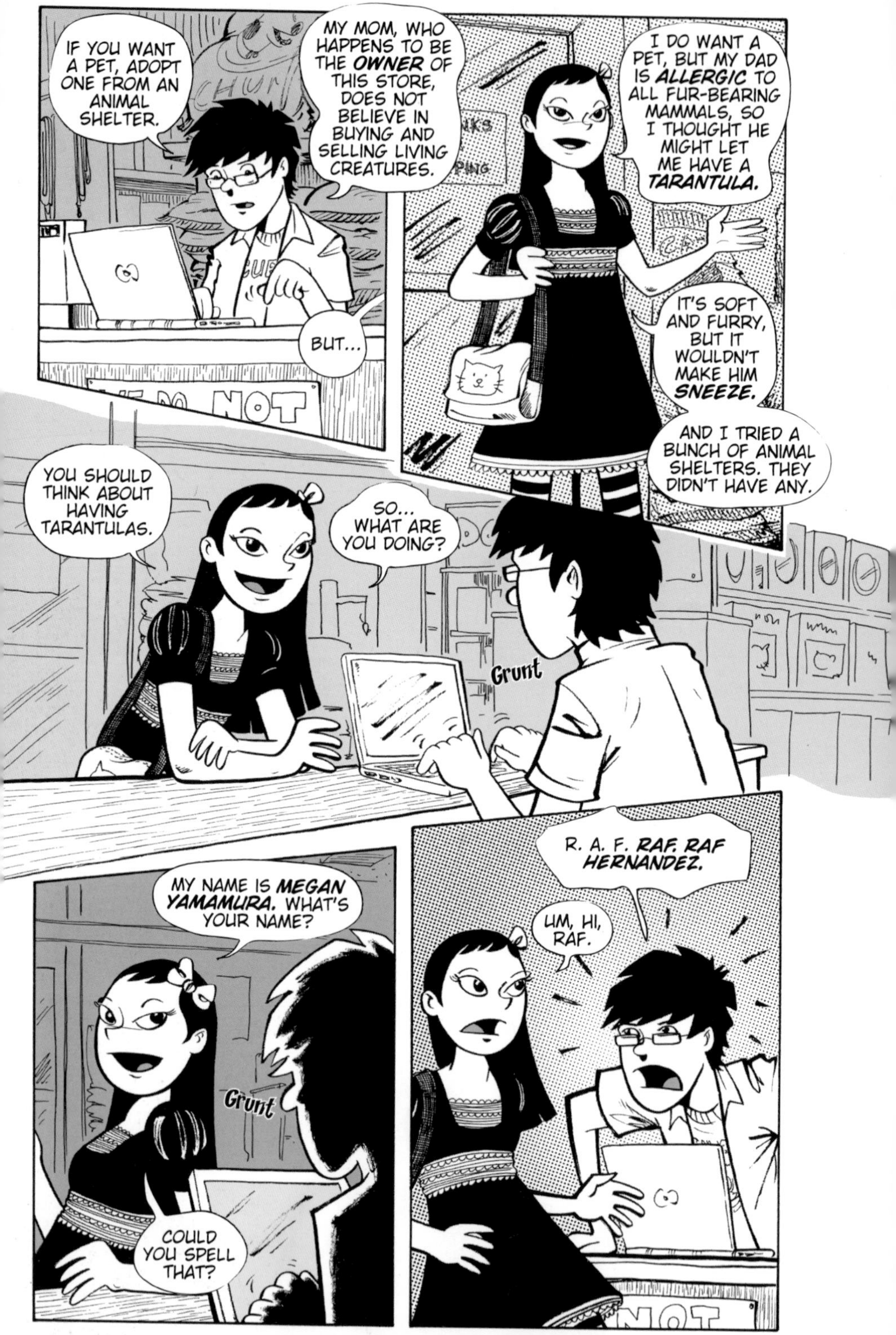

IF YOU WANT A PET, ADOPT ONE FROM AN ANIMAL SHELTER.
MY MOM, WHO HAPPENS TO BE THE OWNER OF THIS STORE, DOES NOT BELIEVE IN BUYING AND SELLING LIVING CREATURES.
BUT...
I DO WANT A PET, BUT MY DAD IS ALLERGIC TO ALL FUR-BEARING MAMMALS, SO I THOUGHT HE MIGHT LET ME HAVE A TARANTULA.
IT'S SOFT AND FURRY, BUT IT WOULDN'T MAKE HIM SNEEZE.
AND I TRIED A BUNCH OF ANIMAL SHELTERS. THEY DIDN'T HAVE ANY.
WE DO NOT
YOU SHOULD THINK ABOUT HAVING TARANTULAS.
SO... WHAT ARE YOU DOING?
Grunt
MY NAME IS MEGAN YAMAMURA. WHAT'S YOUR NAME?
Grunt
COULD YOU SPELL THAT?
R. A. F. RAF. RAF HERNANDEZ.
UM, HI, RAF.
NOT

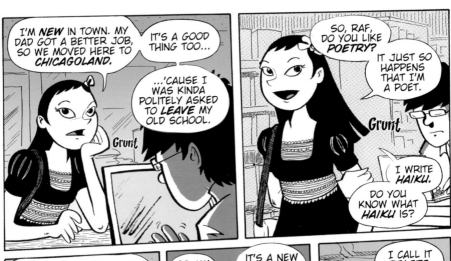

I'M **NEW** IN TOWN. MY DAD GOT A BETTER JOB, SO WE MOVED HERE TO **CHICAGOLAND**.

IT'S A GOOD THING TOO...

...'CAUSE I WAS KINDA POLITELY ASKED TO **LEAVE** MY OLD SCHOOL.

Grunt

SO, RAF, DO YOU LIKE **POETRY**?

IT JUST SO HAPPENS THAT I'M A POET.

Grunt

I WRITE **HAIKU**.

DO YOU KNOW WHAT **HAIKU** IS?

IT'S A KIND OF **JAPANESE POETRY** THAT CONSISTS OF THREE LINES OF FIVE, SEVEN, AND FIVE SYLLABLES.

Grunt

SO, UM, WHAT'S THAT?

IT'S A NEW **PROGRAM** I'M INVENTING, AND IT'S **WAY MORE** THAN JUST A PROGRAM.

I CALL IT **DELETE**, AS IN...

LIKE:
WHAT ARE YOU MISSING
HIDING BEHIND YOUR SMALL SCREEN?
THERE'S A WORLD OUT THERE.

AMSCRAY, GO AWAY, AND DON'T LET THE DOOR HIT YOU ON THE WAY OUT!!!

OKAY, I CAN TAKE A HINT.

JEEZ! TARANTULAS!

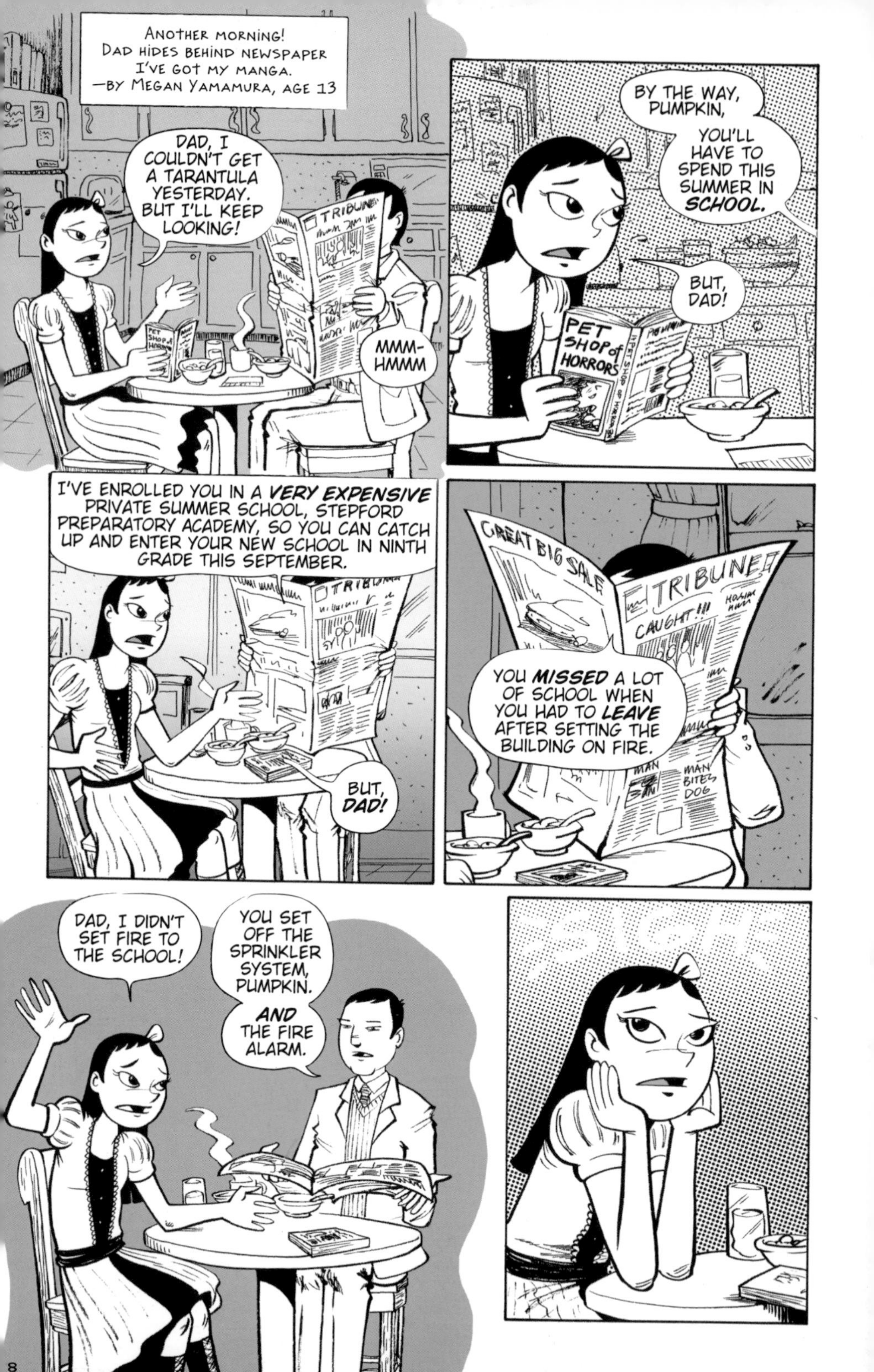
ANOTHER MORNING!
DAD HIDES BEHIND NEWSPAPER
I'VE GOT MY MANGA.
—BY MEGAN YAMAMURA, AGE 13
DAD, I COULDN'T GET A TARANTULA YESTERDAY. BUT I'LL KEEP LOOKING!
MMM-HMMM
BY THE WAY, PUMPKIN,
YOU'LL HAVE TO SPEND THIS SUMMER IN SCHOOL.
BUT, DAD!
PET SHOP of HORRORS
I'VE ENROLLED YOU IN A VERY EXPENSIVE PRIVATE SUMMER SCHOOL, STEPFORD PREPARATORY ACADEMY, SO YOU CAN CATCH UP AND ENTER YOUR NEW SCHOOL IN NINTH GRADE THIS SEPTEMBER.
BUT, DAD!
GREAT BIG SALE
TRIBUNE
CAUGHT!!!
YOU MISSED A LOT OF SCHOOL WHEN YOU HAD TO LEAVE AFTER SETTING THE BUILDING ON FIRE.
MAN BITES DOG
DAD, I DIDN'T SET FIRE TO THE SCHOOL!
YOU SET OFF THE SPRINKLER SYSTEM, PUMPKIN.
AND THE FIRE ALARM.
SIGH

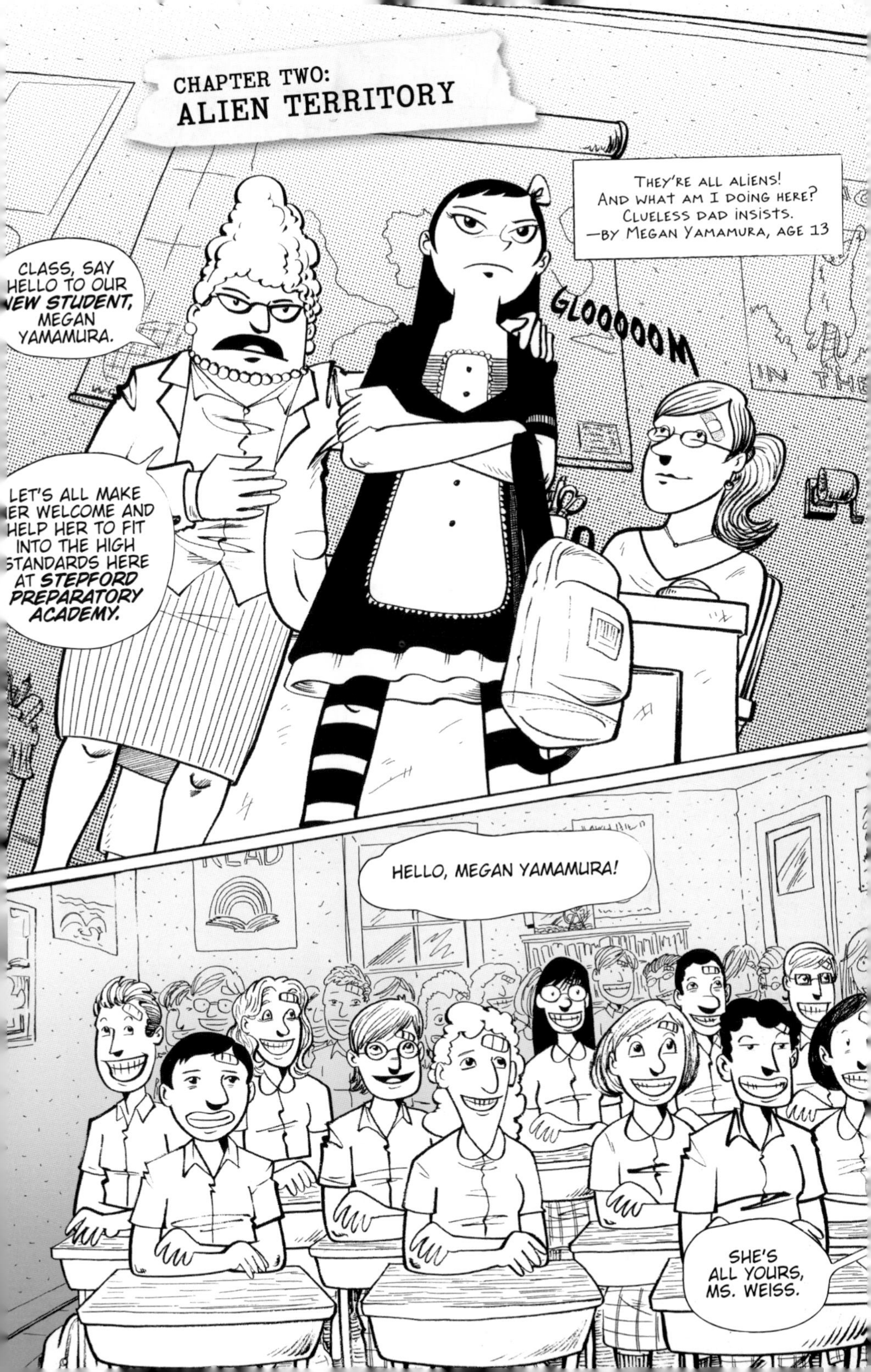

CHAPTER TWO:
ALIEN TERRITORY
THEY'RE ALL ALIENS! AND WHAT AM I DOING HERE? CLUELESS DAD INSISTS. —BY MEGAN YAMAMURA, AGE 13
CLASS, SAY HELLO TO OUR ***EW STUDENT,*** MEGAN YAMAMURA.
GLOOOOOM
LET'S ALL MAKE ER WELCOME AND HELP HER TO FIT INTO THE HIGH STANDARDS HERE AT ***STEPFORD PREPARATORY ACADEMY.***
HELLO, MEGAN YAMAMURA!
SHE'S ALL YOURS, MS. WEISS.

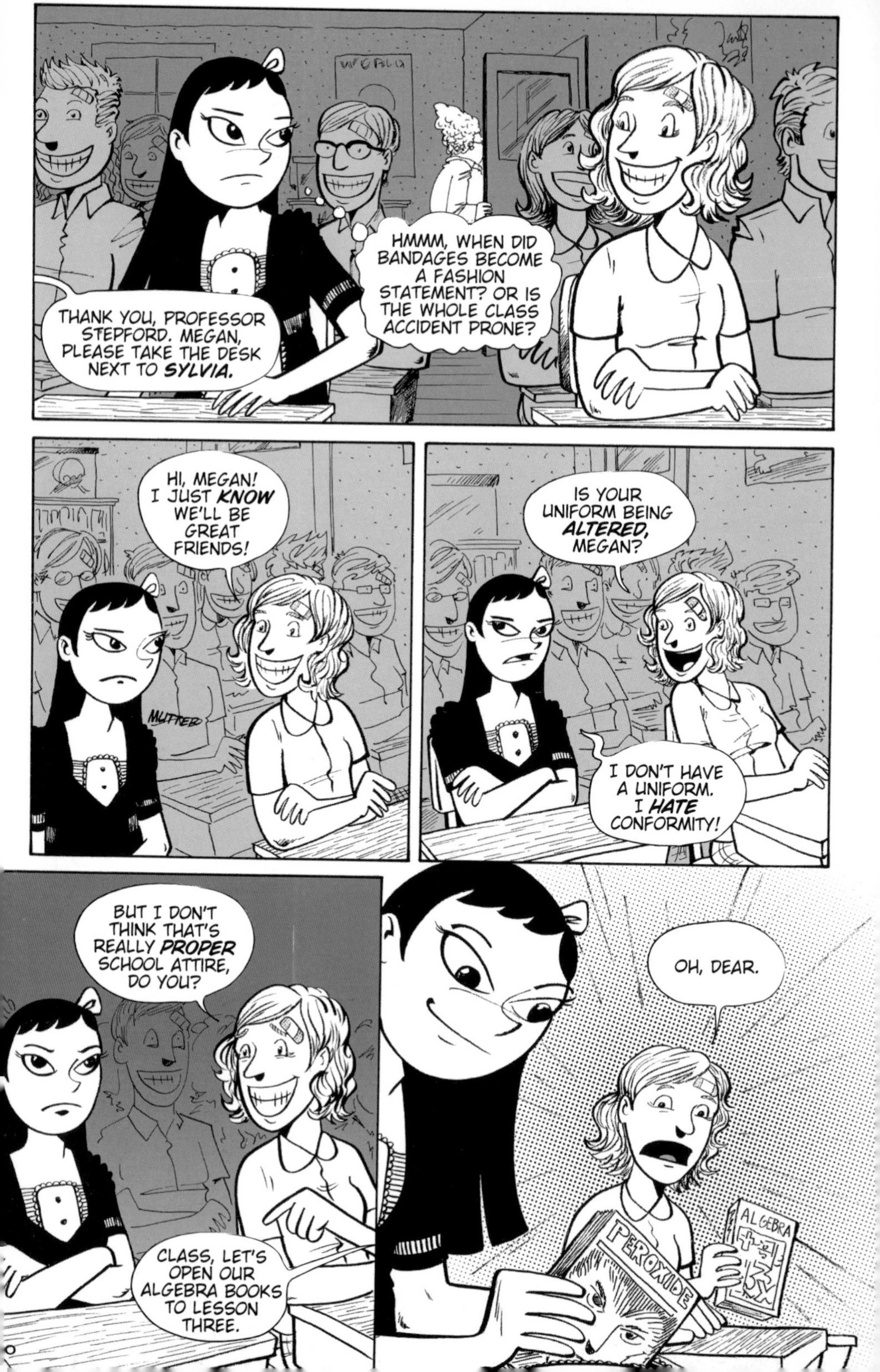
THANK YOU, PROFESSOR STEPFORD. MEGAN, PLEASE TAKE THE DESK NEXT TO **SYLVIA.**
HMMM, WHEN DID BANDAGES BECOME A FASHION STATEMENT? OR IS THE WHOLE CLASS ACCIDENT PRONE?
HI, MEGAN! I JUST **KNOW** WE'LL BE GREAT FRIENDS!
MUTTER
IS YOUR UNIFORM BEING **ALTERED,** MEGAN?
I DON'T HAVE A UNIFORM. I **HATE** CONFORMITY!
BUT I DON'T THINK THAT'S REALLY **PROPER** SCHOOL ATTIRE, DO YOU?
CLASS, LET'S OPEN OUR ALGEBRA BOOKS TO LESSON THREE.
OH, DEAR.
PEROXIDE
ALGEBRA

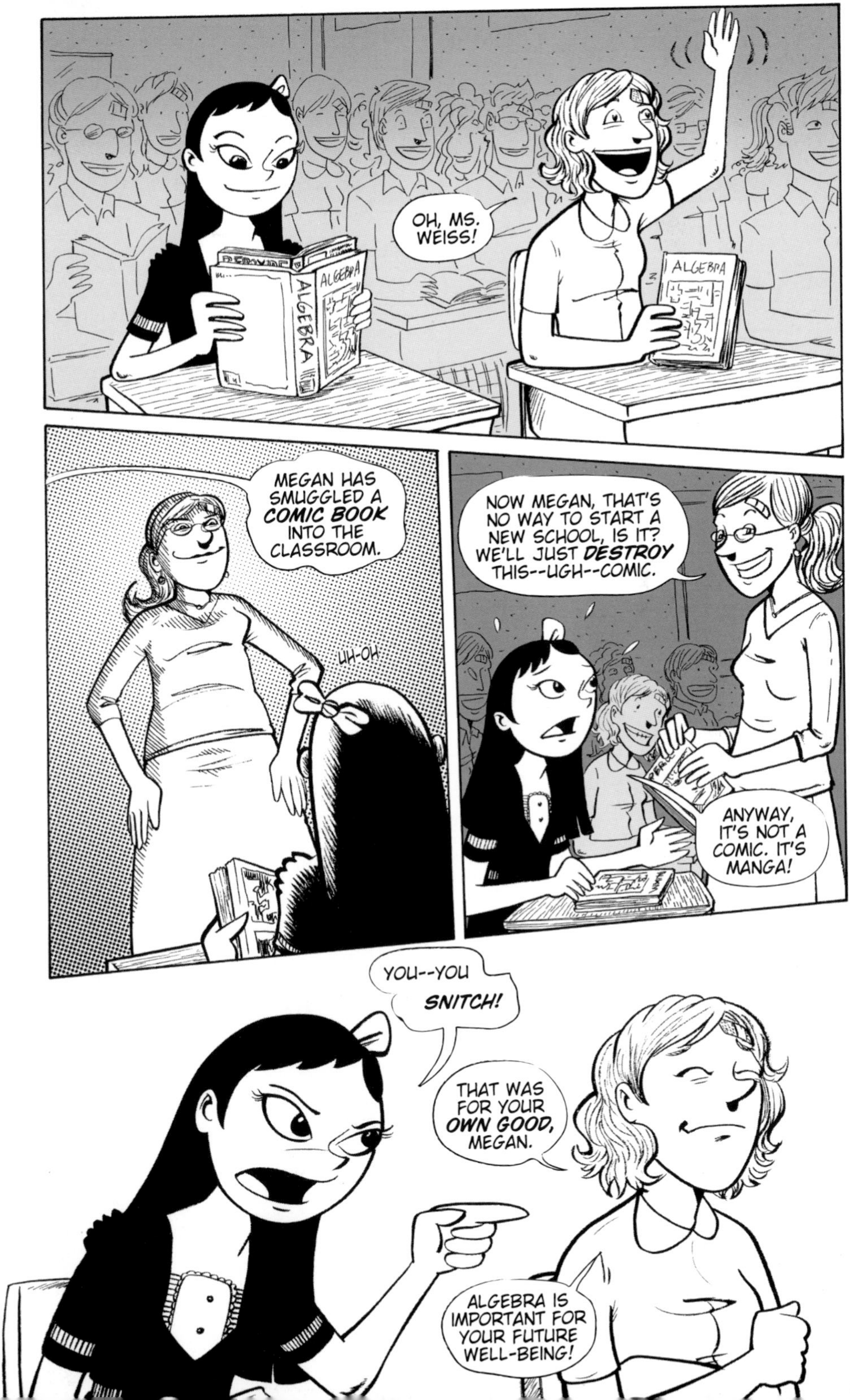
OH, MS. WEISS!
MEGAN HAS SMUGGLED A *COMIC BOOK* INTO THE CLASSROOM.
UH-OH
NOW MEGAN, THAT'S NO WAY TO START A NEW SCHOOL, IS IT? WE'LL JUST *DESTROY* THIS--UGH--COMIC.
ANYWAY, IT'S NOT A COMIC. IT'S MANGA!
YOU--YOU *SNITCH!*
THAT WAS FOR YOUR *OWN GOOD,* MEGAN.
ALGEBRA IS IMPORTANT FOR YOUR FUTURE WELL-BEING!

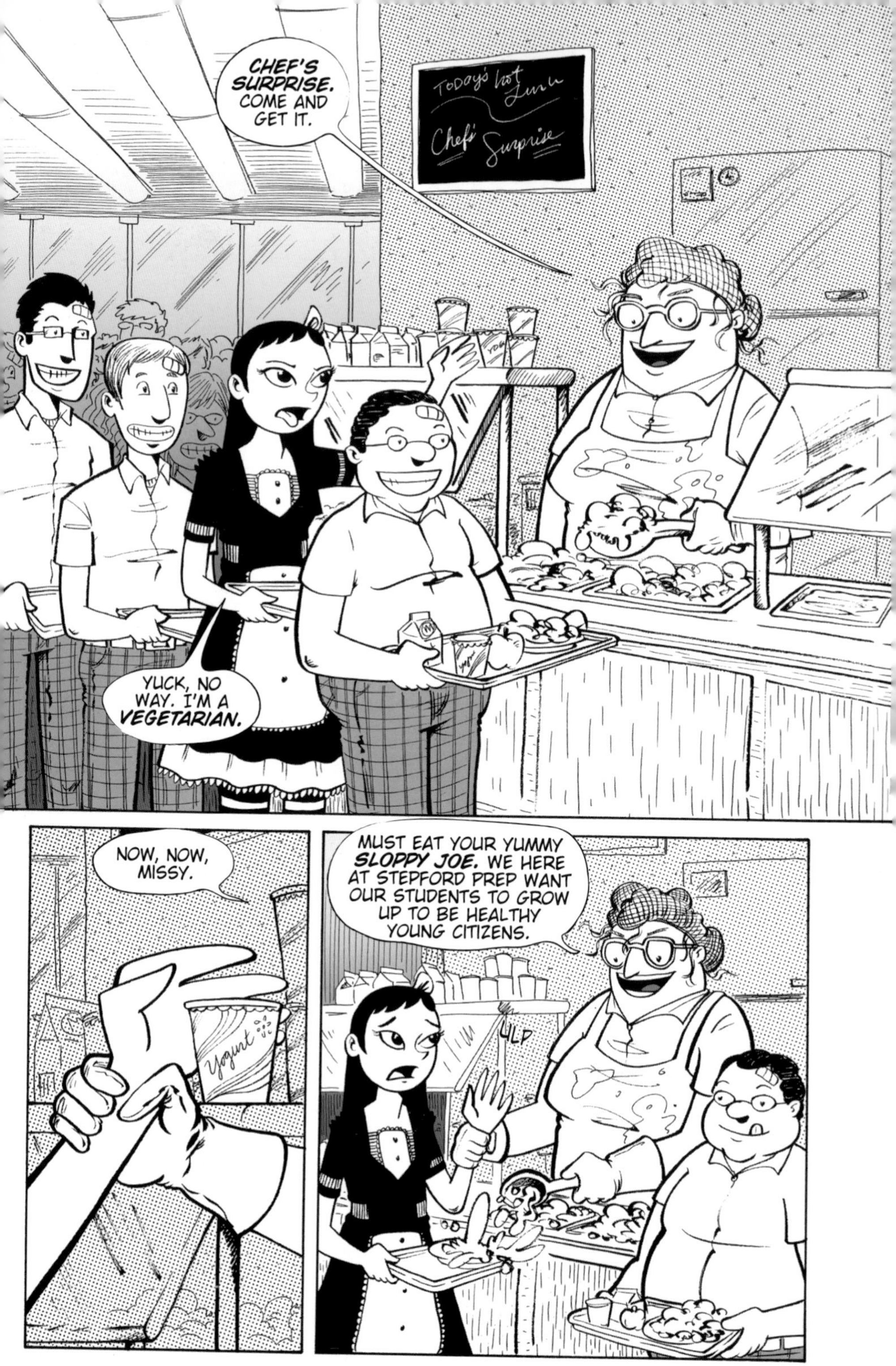

CHEF'S SURPRISE. COME AND GET IT.
Today's hot Lunch
Chef's Surprise
YUCK, NO WAY. I'M A VEGETARIAN.
NOW, NOW, MISSY.
Yogurt
MUST EAT YOUR YUMMY SLOPPY JOE. WE HERE AT STEPFORD PREP WANT OUR STUDENTS TO GROW UP TO BE HEALTHY YOUNG CITIZENS.
ULP

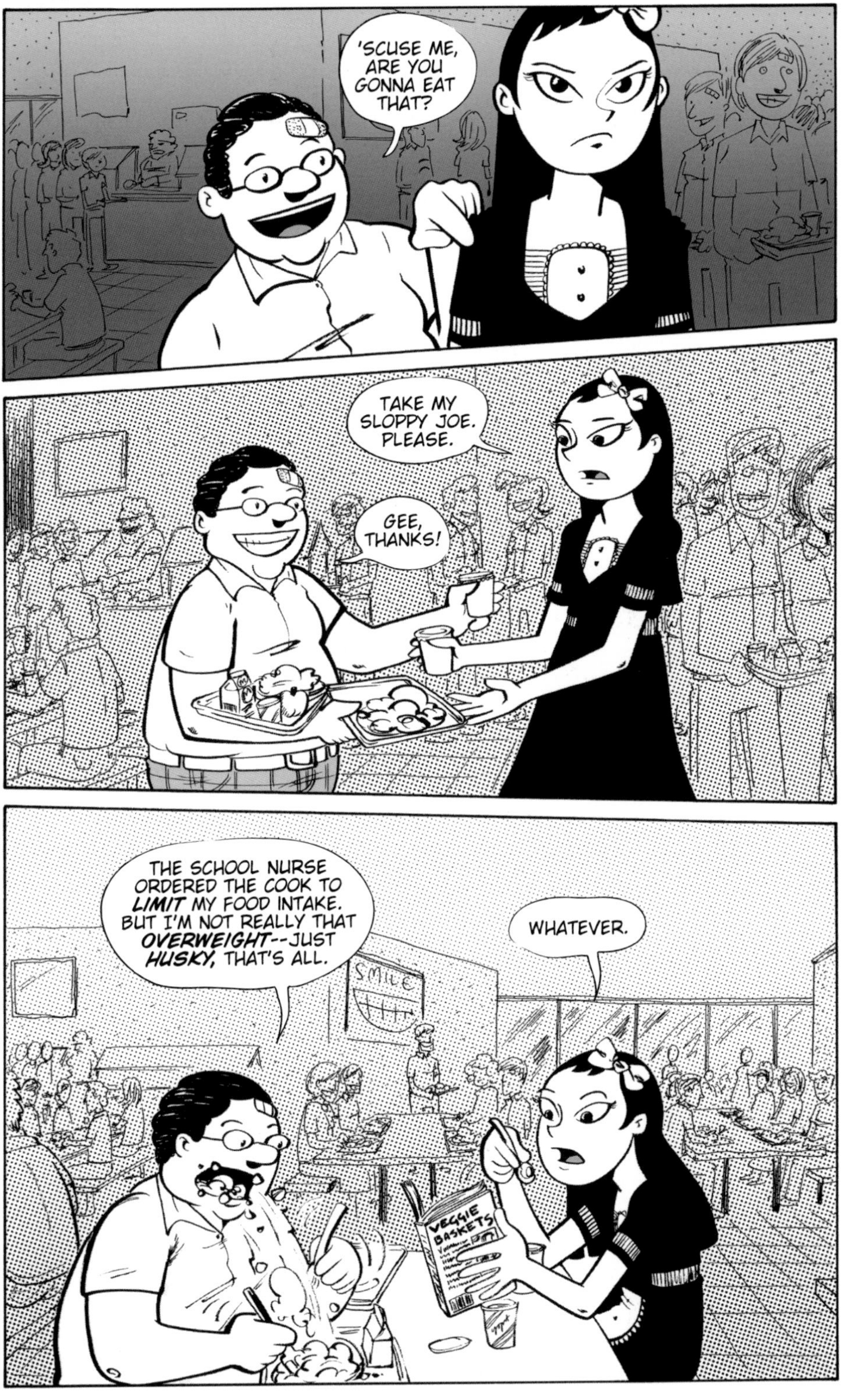
'SCUSE ME, ARE YOU GONNA EAT THAT?
TAKE MY SLOPPY JOE. PLEASE.
GEE, THANKS!
THE SCHOOL NURSE ORDERED THE COOK TO *LIMIT* MY FOOD INTAKE. BUT I'M NOT REALLY THAT *OVERWEIGHT*--JUST *HUSKY,* THAT'S ALL.
WHATEVER.
SMILE
VEGGIE BASKETS

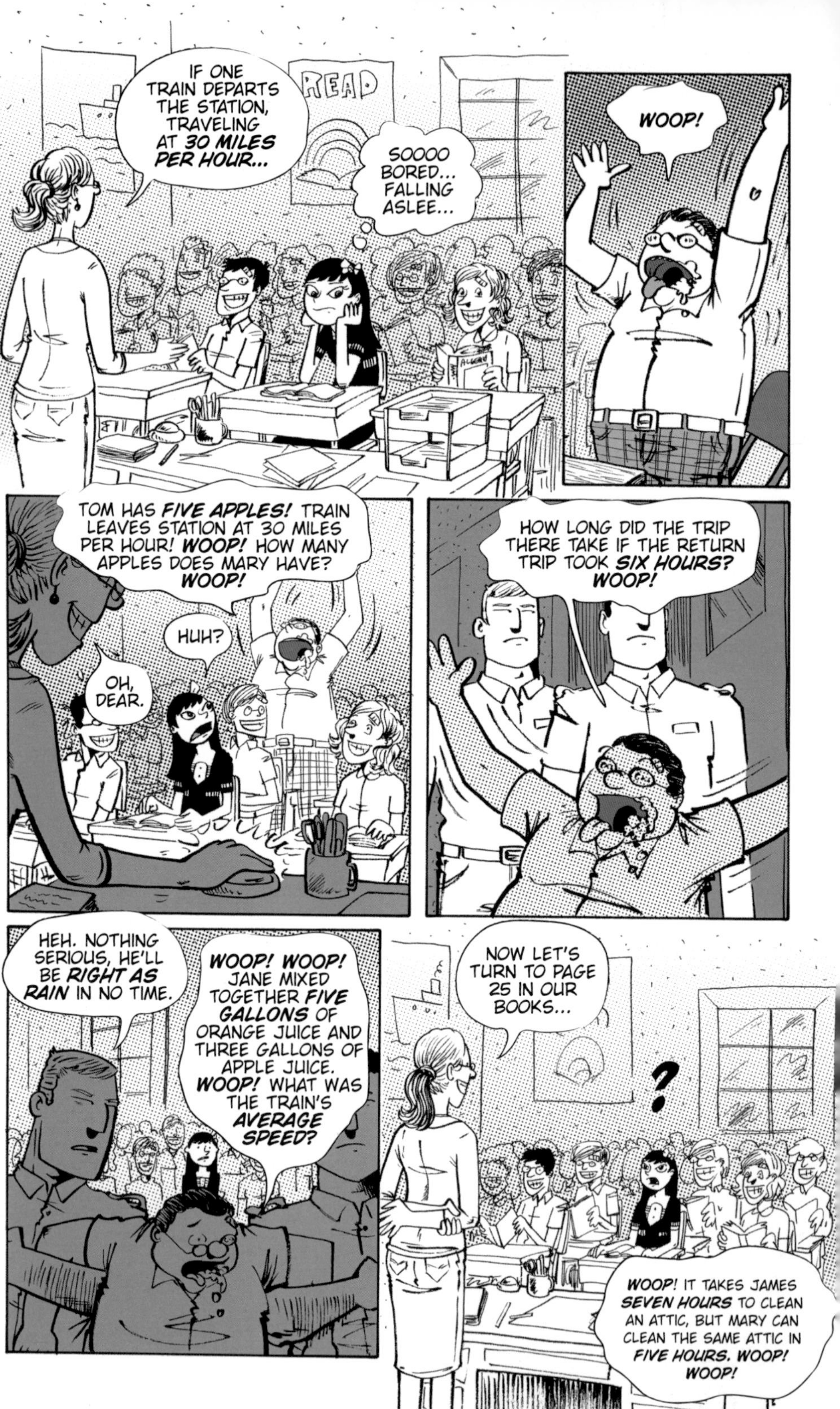
IF ONE TRAIN DEPARTS THE STATION, TRAVELING AT 30 MILES PER HOUR...
READ
SOOOO BORED... FALLING ASLEE...
WOOP!
TOM HAS FIVE APPLES! TRAIN LEAVES STATION AT 30 MILES PER HOUR! WOOP! HOW MANY APPLES DOES MARY HAVE? WOOP!
HUH?
OH, DEAR.
HOW LONG DID THE TRIP THERE TAKE IF THE RETURN TRIP TOOK SIX HOURS? WOOP!
HEH. NOTHING SERIOUS, HE'LL BE RIGHT AS RAIN IN NO TIME.
WOOP! WOOP! JANE MIXED TOGETHER FIVE GALLONS OF ORANGE JUICE AND THREE GALLONS OF APPLE JUICE. WOOP! WHAT WAS THE TRAIN'S AVERAGE SPEED?
NOW LET'S TURN TO PAGE 25 IN OUR BOOKS...
?
WOOP! IT TAKES JAMES SEVEN HOURS TO CLEAN AN ATTIC, BUT MARY CAN CLEAN THE SAME ATTIC IN FIVE HOURS. WOOP! WOOP!

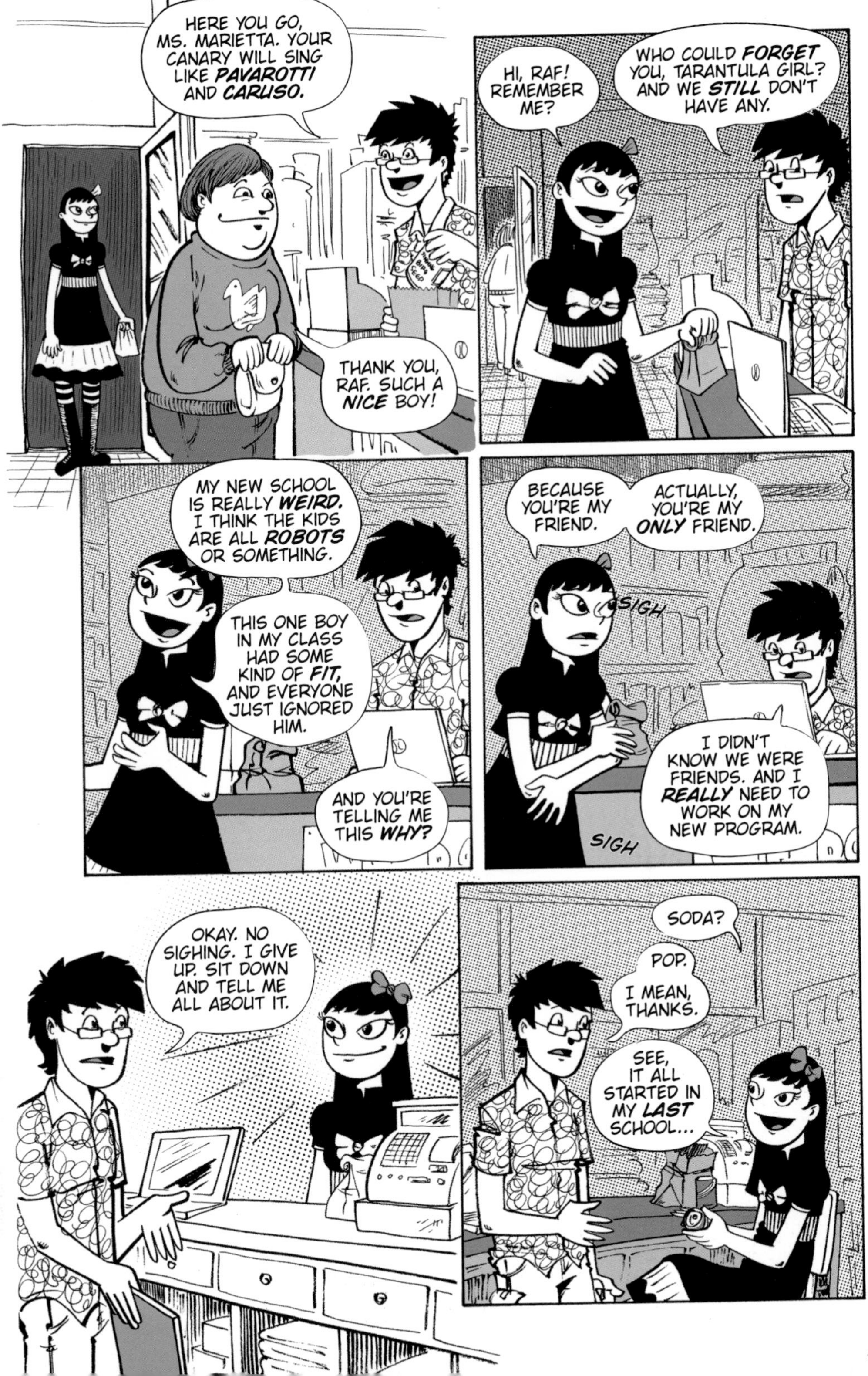
HERE YOU GO, MS. MARIETTA. YOUR CANARY WILL SING LIKE PAVAROTTI AND CARUSO.
THANK YOU, RAF. SUCH A NICE BOY!
HI, RAF! REMEMBER ME?
WHO COULD FORGET YOU, TARANTULA GIRL? AND WE STILL DON'T HAVE ANY.
MY NEW SCHOOL IS REALLY WEIRD. I THINK THE KIDS ARE ALL ROBOTS OR SOMETHING.
THIS ONE BOY IN MY CLASS HAD SOME KIND OF FIT, AND EVERYONE JUST IGNORED HIM.
AND YOU'RE TELLING ME THIS WHY?
BECAUSE YOU'RE MY FRIEND.
ACTUALLY, YOU'RE MY ONLY FRIEND.
SIGH
I DIDN'T KNOW WE WERE FRIENDS. AND I REALLY NEED TO WORK ON MY NEW PROGRAM.
SIGH
OKAY. NO SIGHING. I GIVE UP. SIT DOWN AND TELL ME ALL ABOUT IT.
SODA?
POP.
I MEAN, THANKS.
SEE, IT ALL STARTED IN MY LAST SCHOOL...

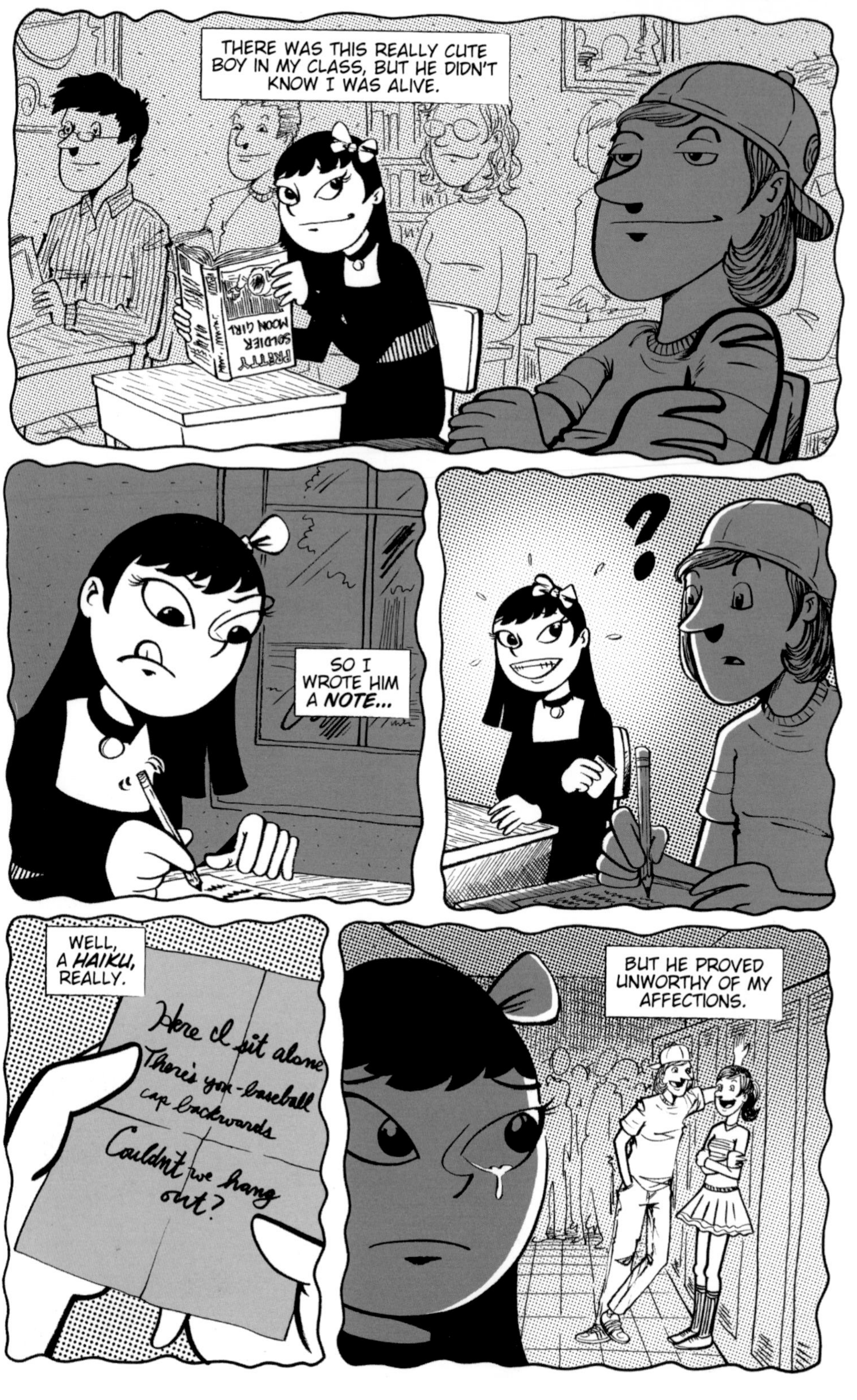
THERE WAS THIS REALLY CUTE BOY IN MY CLASS, BUT HE DIDN'T KNOW I WAS ALIVE.
PRETTY SOLDIER MOON GIRL
SO I WROTE HIM A NOTE...
?
WELL, A HAIKU, REALLY.
Here I sit alone
There's you—baseball cap backwards
Couldn't we hang out?
BUT HE PROVED UNWORTHY OF MY AFFECTIONS.

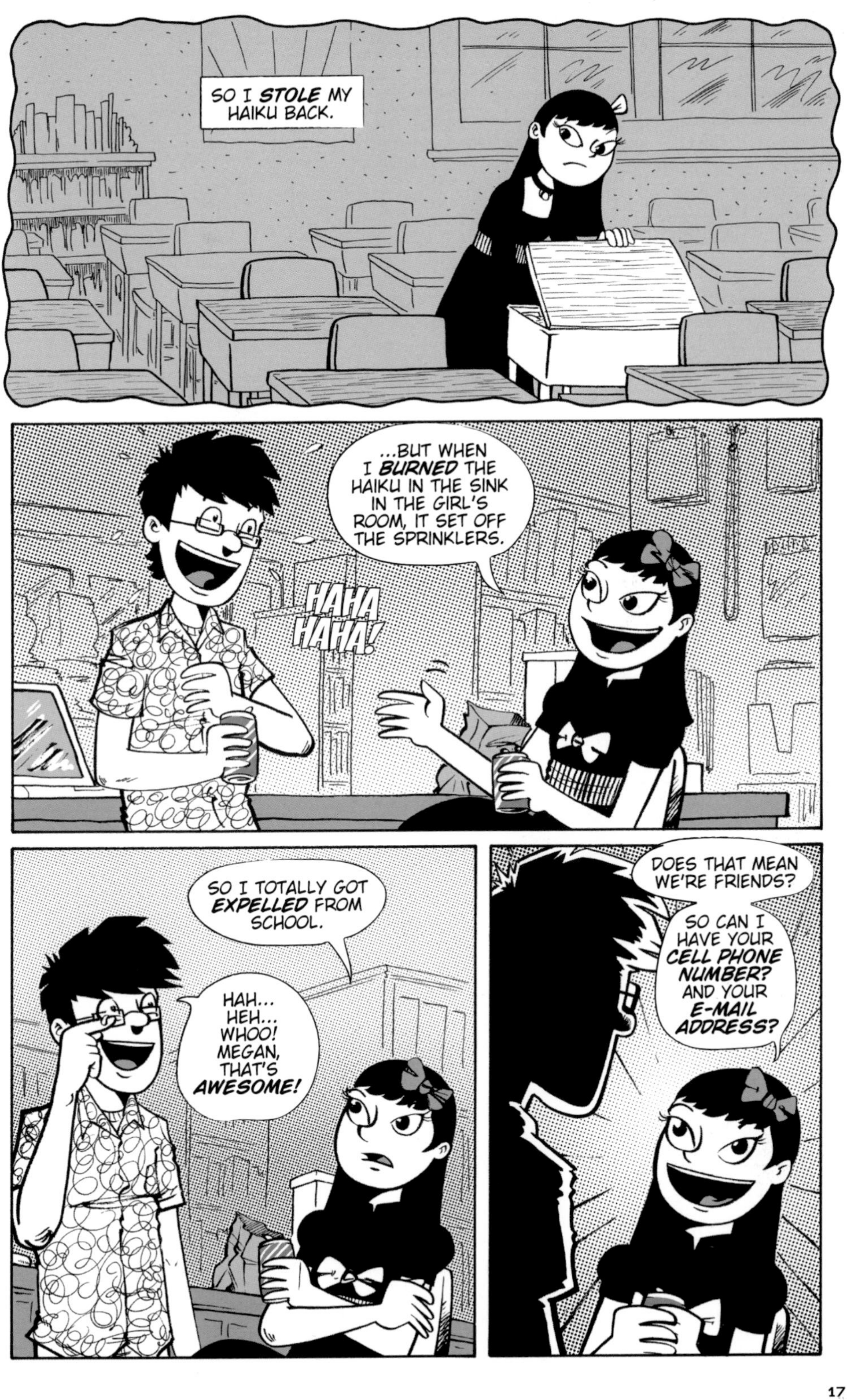
SO I STOLE MY HAIKU BACK.
...BUT WHEN I BURNED THE HAIKU IN THE SINK IN THE GIRL'S ROOM, IT SET OFF THE SPRINKLERS.
HAHA HAHA!
SO I TOTALLY GOT EXPELLED FROM SCHOOL.
HAH... HEH... WHOO! MEGAN, THAT'S AWESOME!
DOES THAT MEAN WE'RE FRIENDS?
SO CAN I HAVE YOUR CELL PHONE NUMBER? AND YOUR E-MAIL ADDRESS?

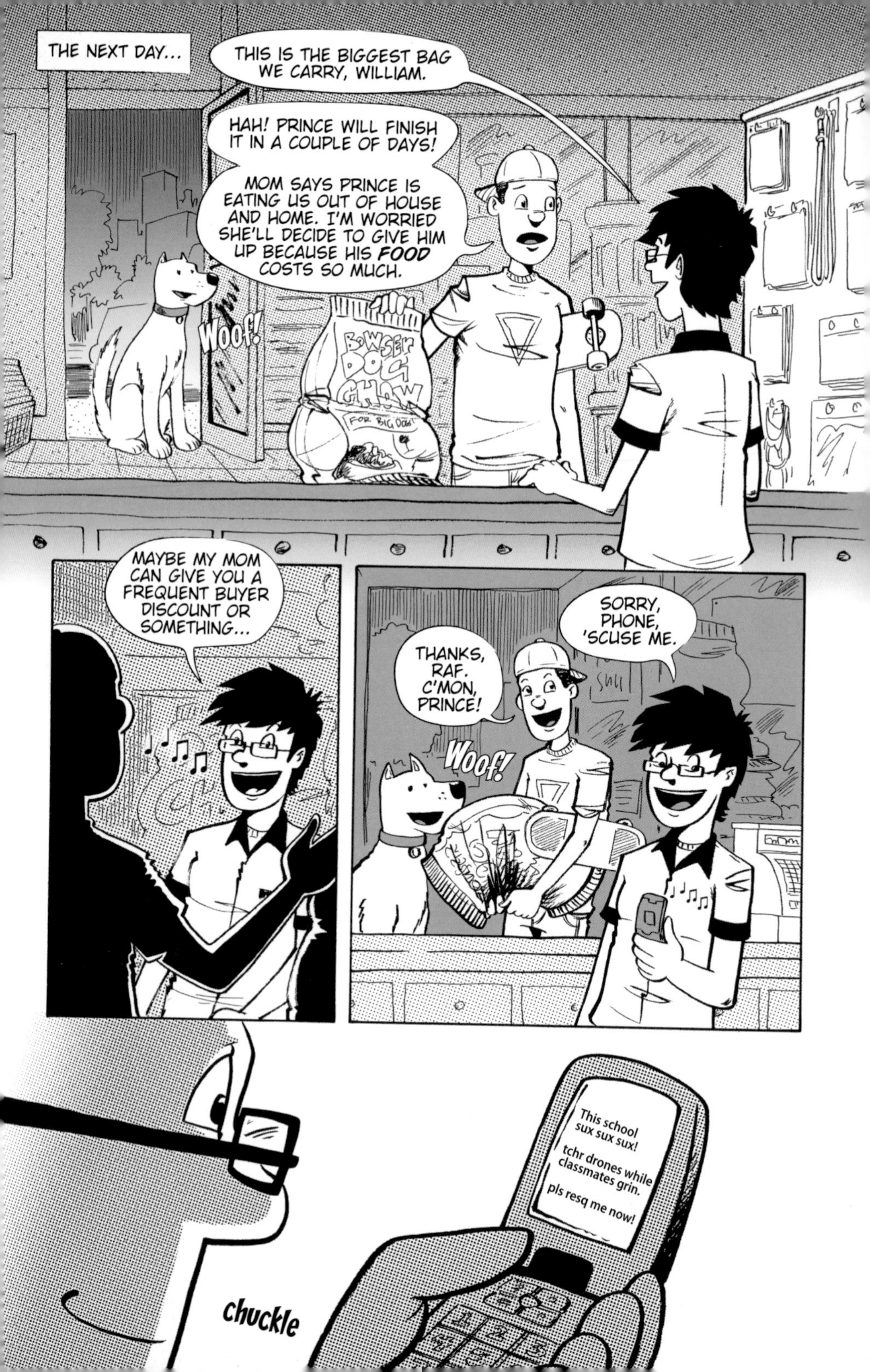
THE NEXT DAY...
THIS IS THE BIGGEST BAG WE CARRY, WILLIAM.
HAH! PRINCE WILL FINISH IT IN A COUPLE OF DAYS!
MOM SAYS PRINCE IS EATING US OUT OF HOUSE AND HOME. I'M WORRIED SHE'LL DECIDE TO GIVE HIM UP BECAUSE HIS FOOD COSTS SO MUCH.
WOOF!
BOWSER DOG CHOW
FOR BIG DOGS!
MAYBE MY MOM CAN GIVE YOU A FREQUENT BUYER DISCOUNT OR SOMETHING...
THANKS, RAF. C'MON, PRINCE!
SORRY, PHONE, 'SCUSE ME.
WOOF!
This school sux sux sux!
tchr drones while classmates grin.
pls resq me now!
chuckle

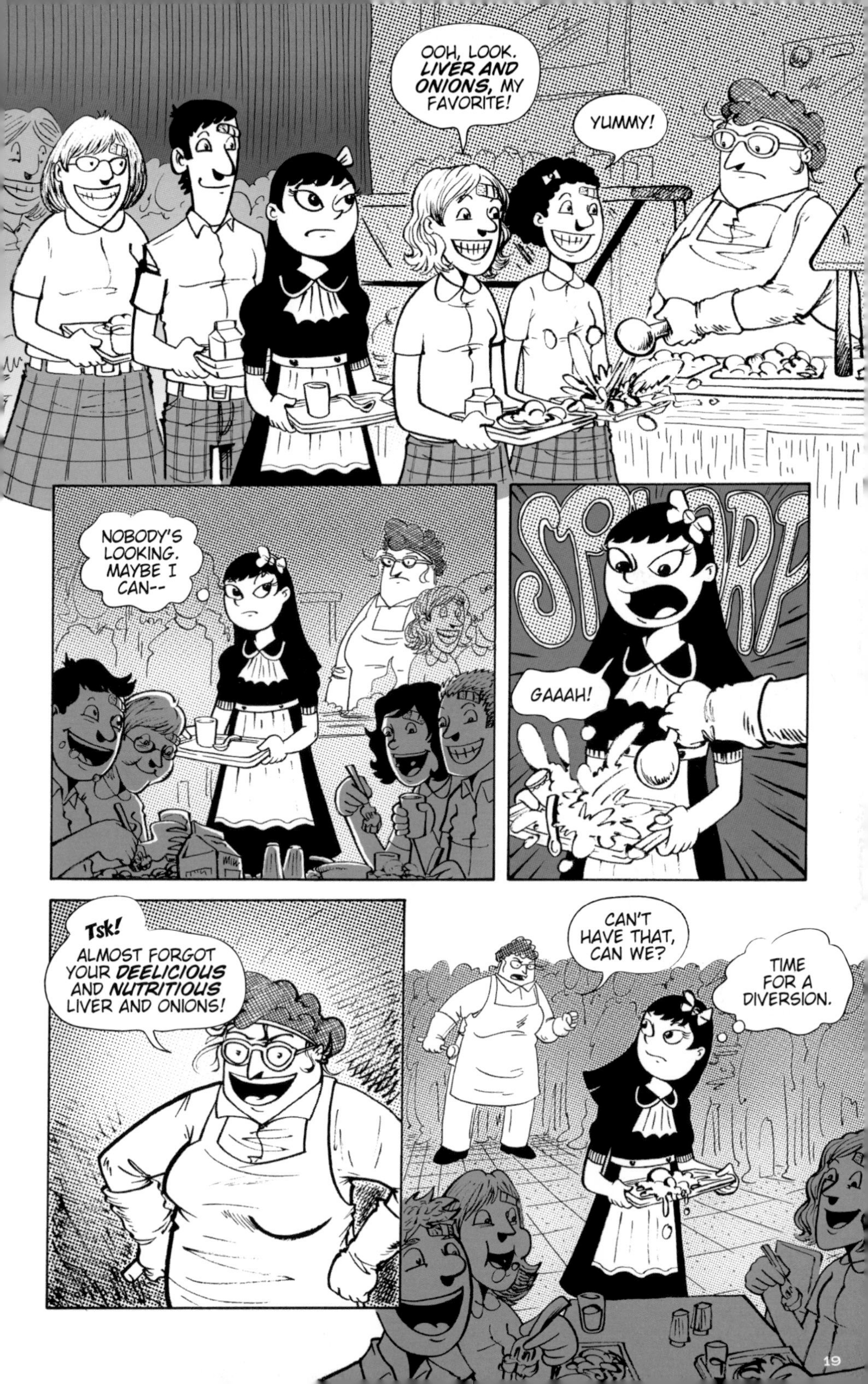
OOH, LOOK. ***LIVER AND ONIONS,*** MY FAVORITE!
YUMMY!
NOBODY'S LOOKING. MAYBE I CAN--
GAAAH!
Tsk! ALMOST FORGOT YOUR ***DEELICIOUS*** AND ***NUTRITIOUS*** LIVER AND ONIONS!
CAN'T HAVE THAT, CAN WE?
TIME FOR A DIVERSION.

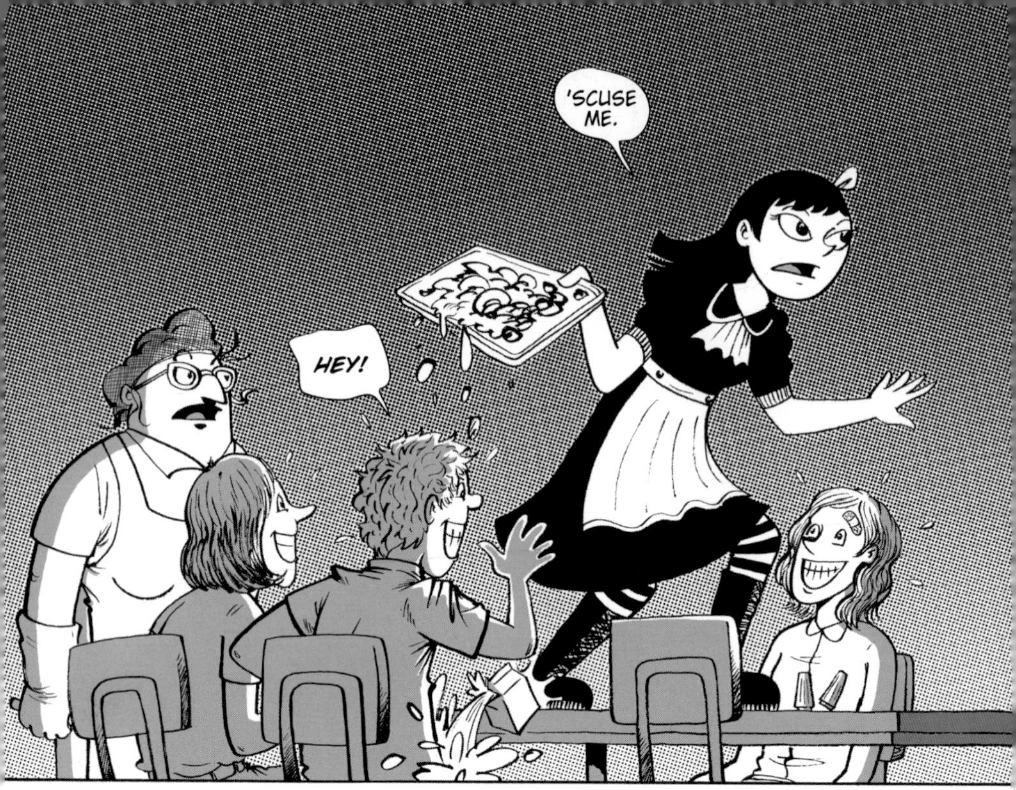
'SCUSE ME.
HEY!

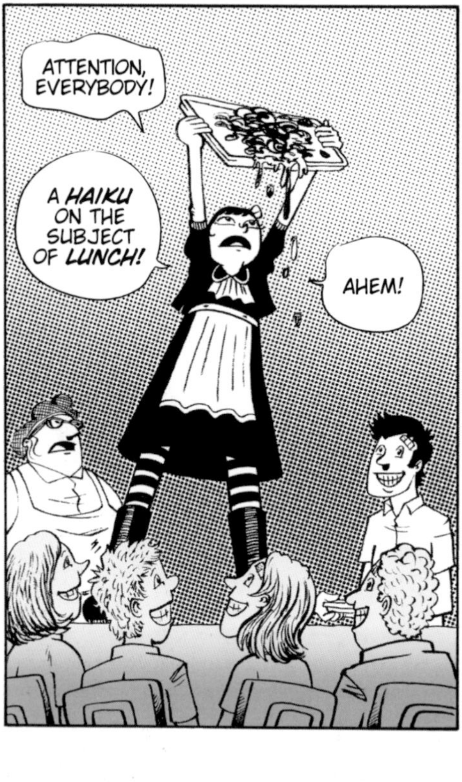
ATTENTION, EVERYBODY!
A *HAIKU* ON THE SUBJECT OF *LUNCH!*
AHEM!

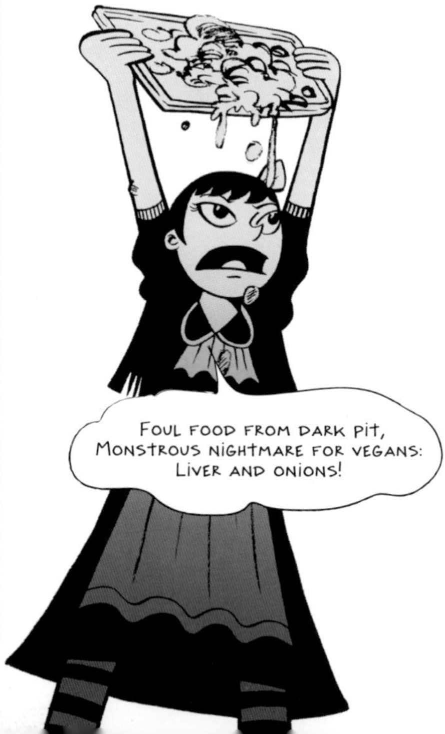
Foul food from dark pit,
Monstrous nightmare for vegans:
Liver and onions!

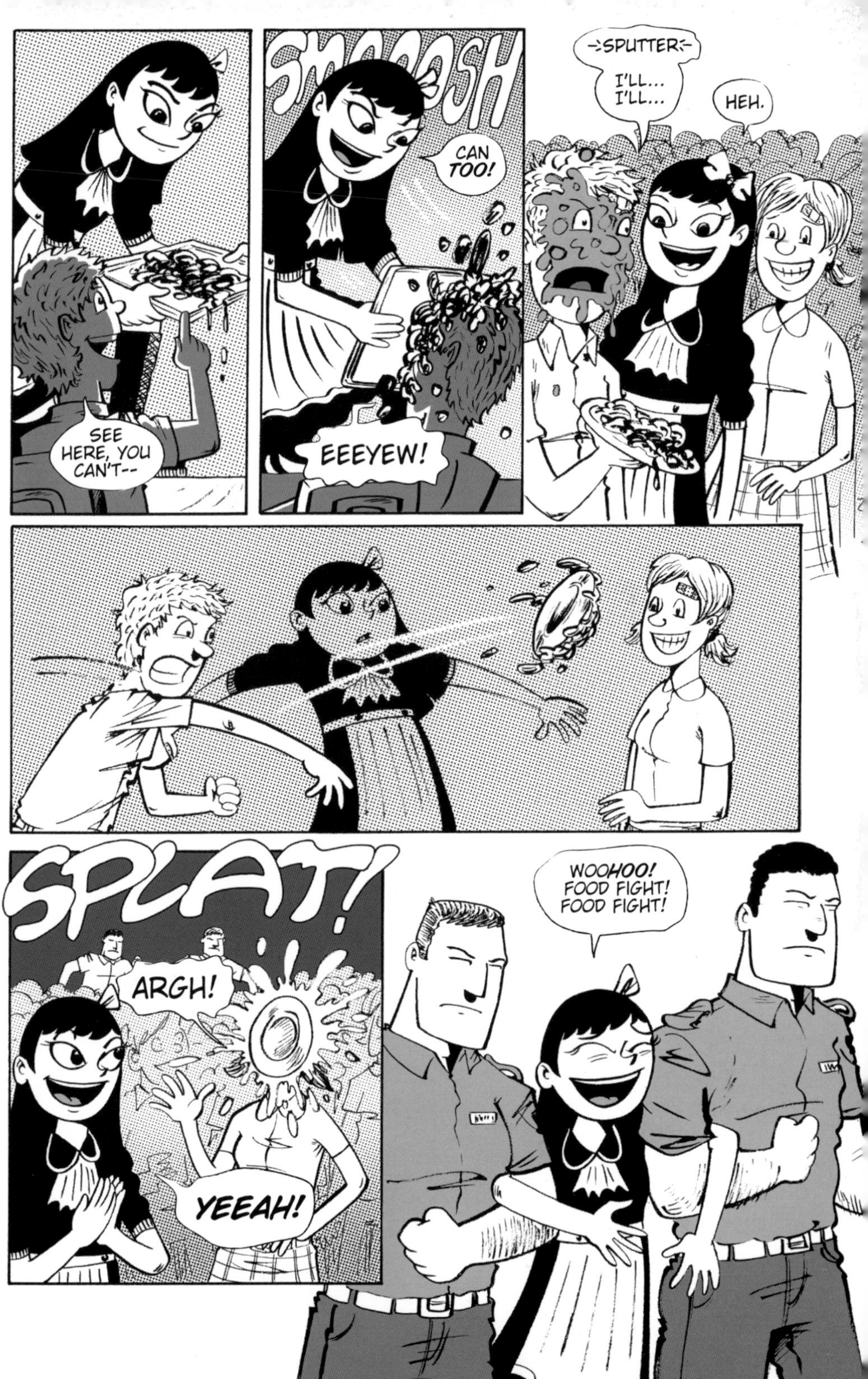
SEE HERE, YOU CAN'T--
SMOOOSH
CAN TOO!
EEEYEW!
-SPUTTER-
I'LL... I'LL...
HEH.
SPLAT!
ARGH!
YEEAH!
WOOHOO! FOOD FIGHT! FOOD FIGHT!

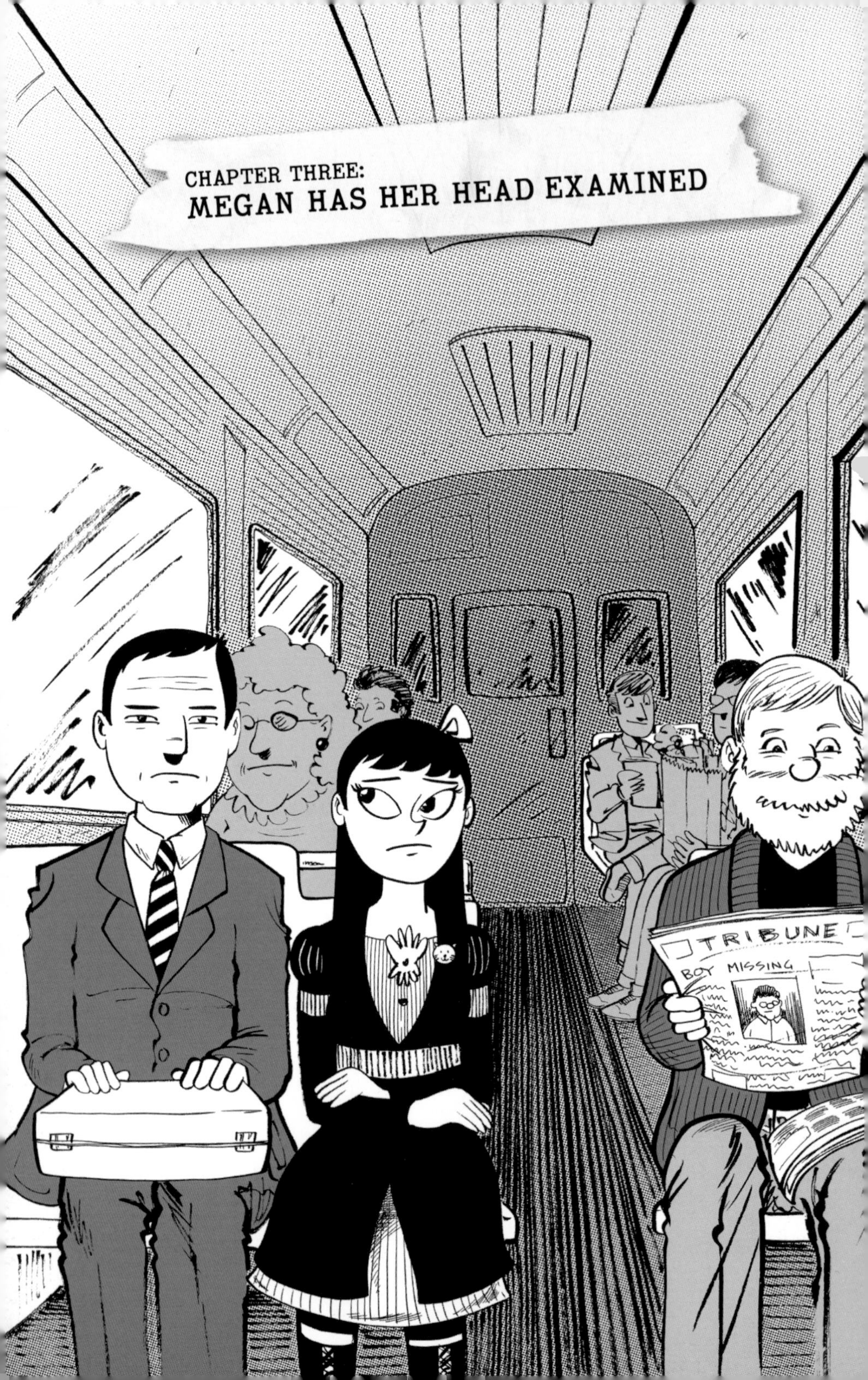
CHAPTER THREE:
MEGAN HAS HER HEAD EXAMINED
TRIBUNE
BOY MISSING

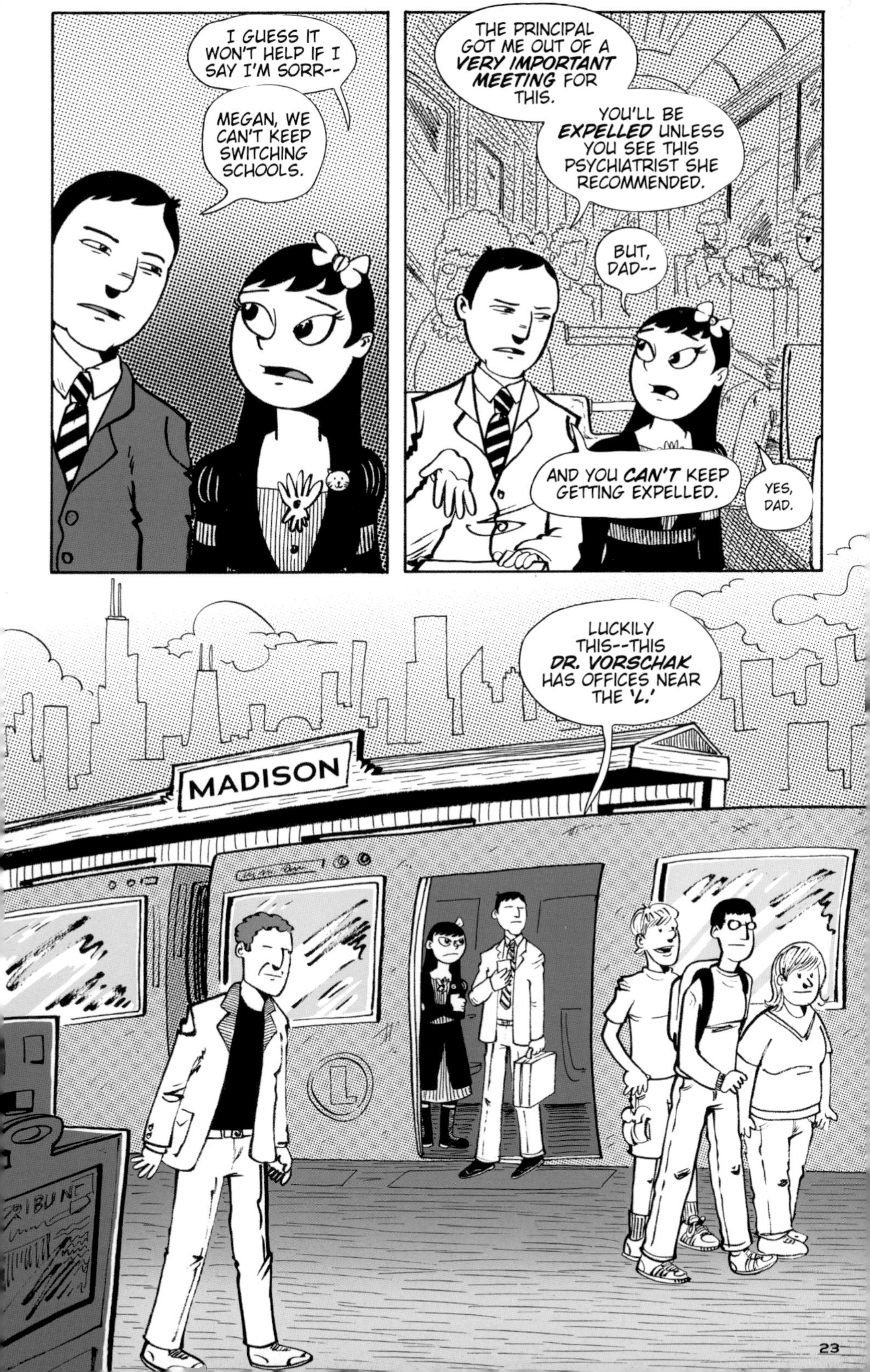
I GUESS IT WON'T HELP IF I SAY I'M SORR--
MEGAN, WE CAN'T KEEP SWITCHING SCHOOLS.
THE PRINCIPAL GOT ME OUT OF A VERY IMPORTANT MEETING FOR THIS.
YOU'LL BE EXPELLED UNLESS YOU SEE THIS PSYCHIATRIST SHE RECOMMENDED.
BUT, DAD--
AND YOU CAN'T KEEP GETTING EXPELLED.
YES, DAD.
LUCKILY THIS--THIS DR. VORSCHAK HAS OFFICES NEAR THE 'L.'
MADISON

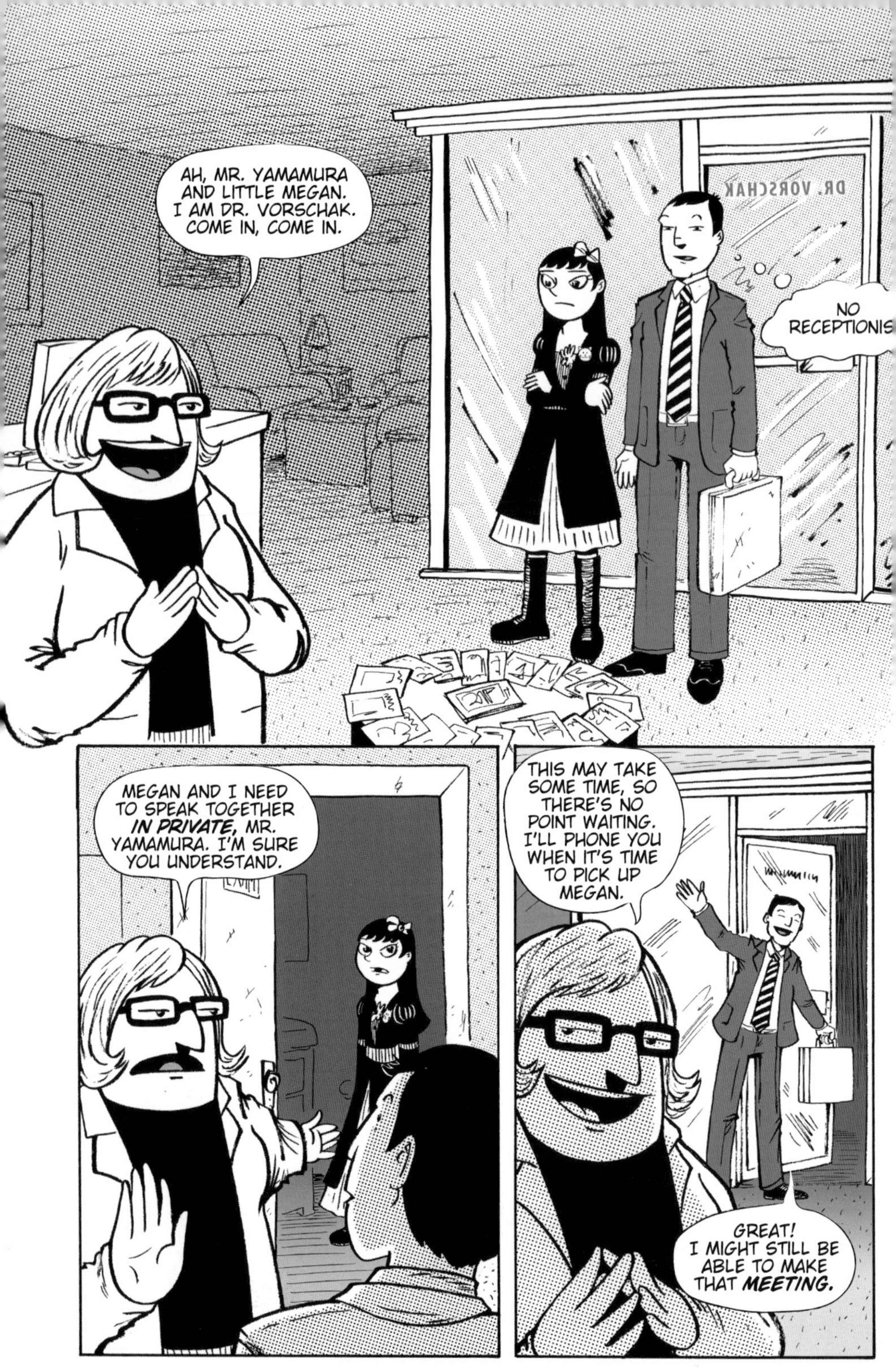
AH, MR. YAMAMURA AND LITTLE MEGAN. I AM DR. VORSCHAK. COME IN, COME IN.
DR. VORSCHAK
NO RECEPTIONIS
MEGAN AND I NEED TO SPEAK TOGETHER ***IN PRIVATE,*** MR. YAMAMURA. I'M SURE YOU UNDERSTAND.
THIS MAY TAKE SOME TIME, SO THERE'S NO POINT WAITING. I'LL PHONE YOU WHEN IT'S TIME TO PICK UP MEGAN.
GREAT! I MIGHT STILL BE ABLE TO MAKE THAT ***MEETING.***

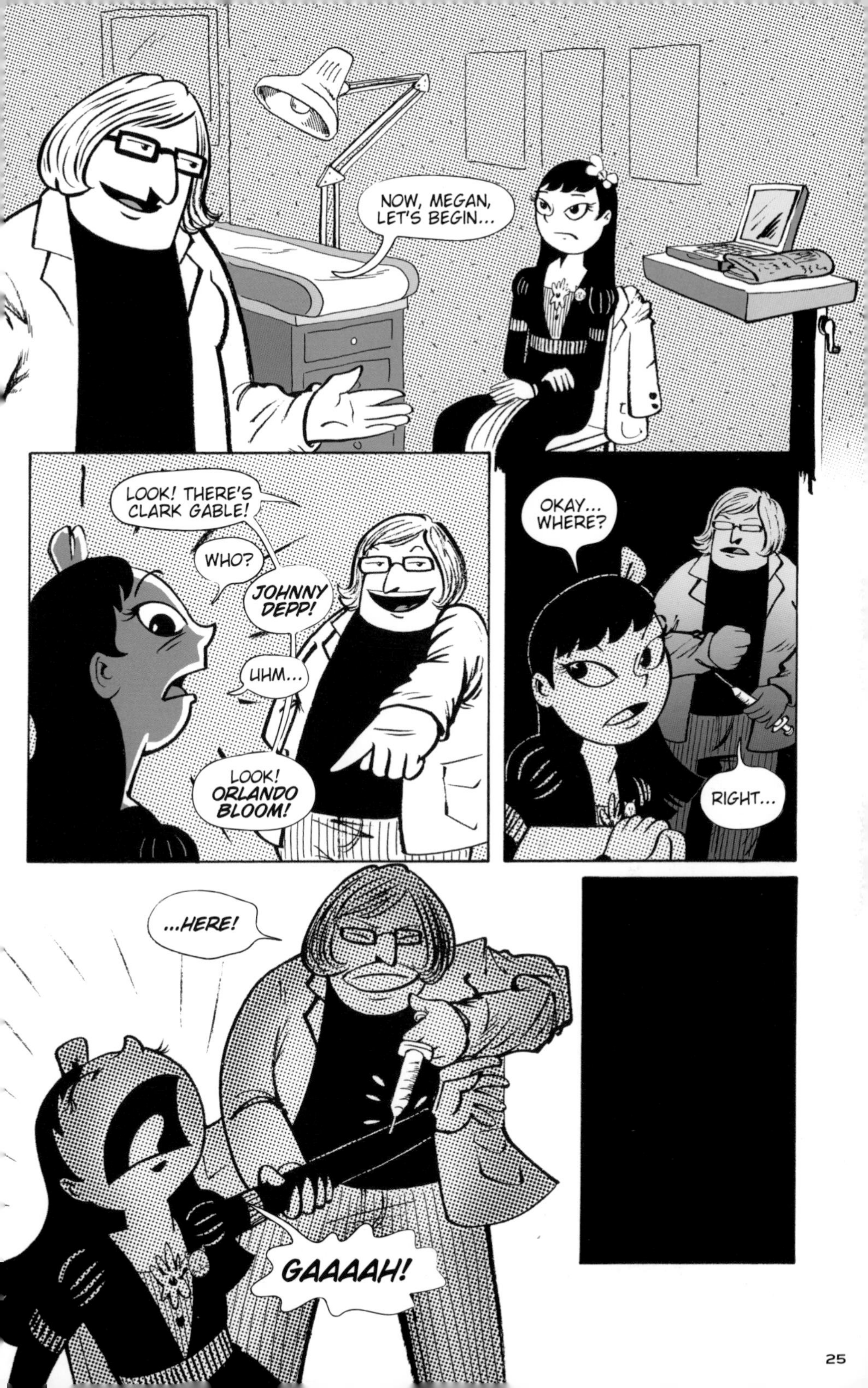
NOW, MEGAN, LET'S BEGIN...
LOOK! THERE'S CLARK GABLE!
WHO?
JOHNNY DEPP!
UHM...
LOOK! ORLANDO BLOOM!
OKAY... WHERE?
RIGHT...
...HERE!
GAAAAH!

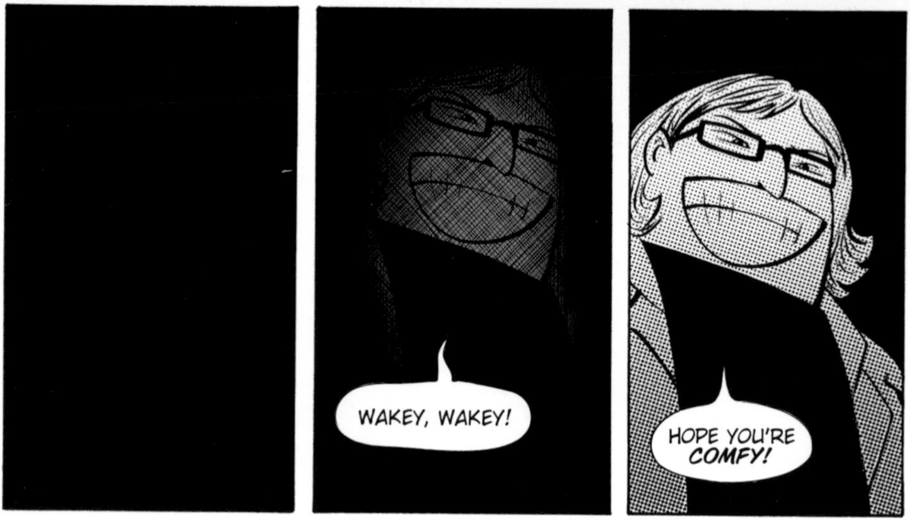
WAKEY, WAKEY!
HOPE YOU'RE COMFY!

CHAPTER FOUR:
THE BRAIN OF A MANIAC!

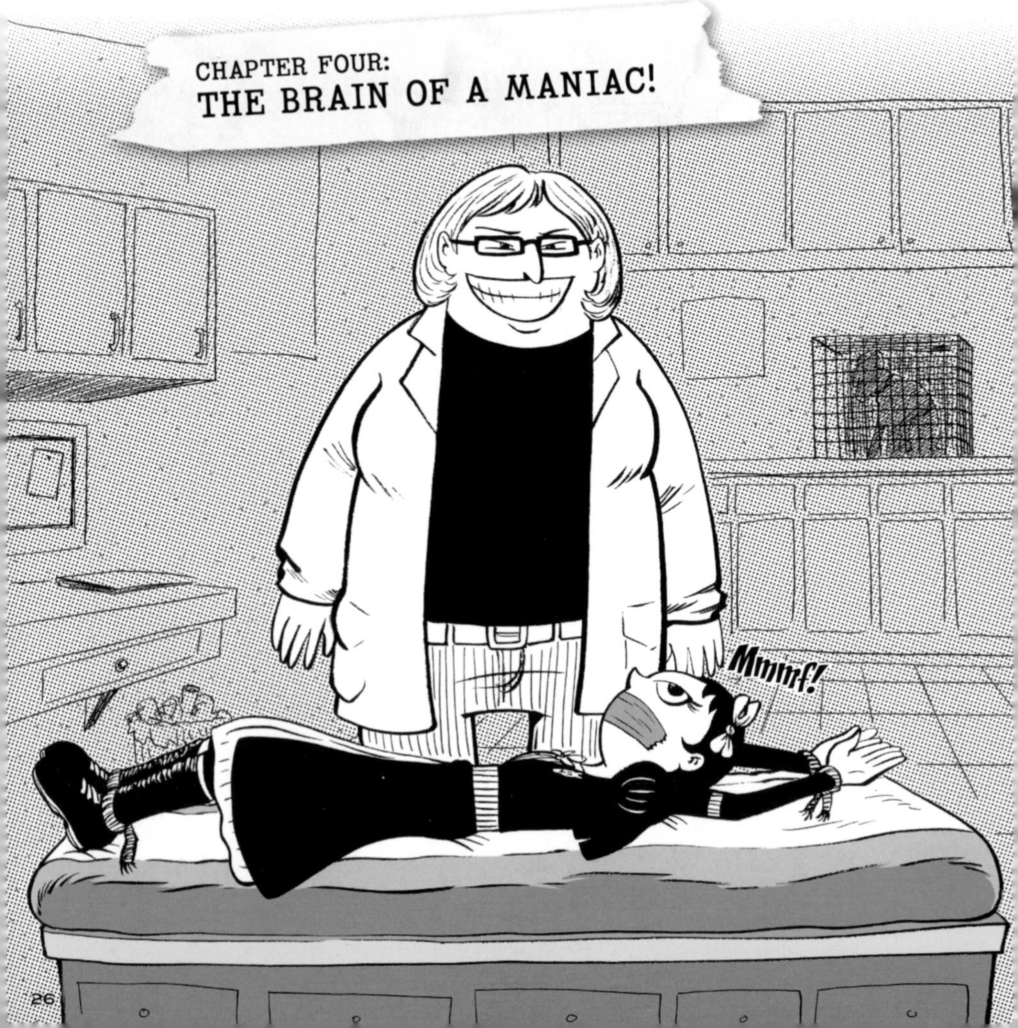
Mmmf!

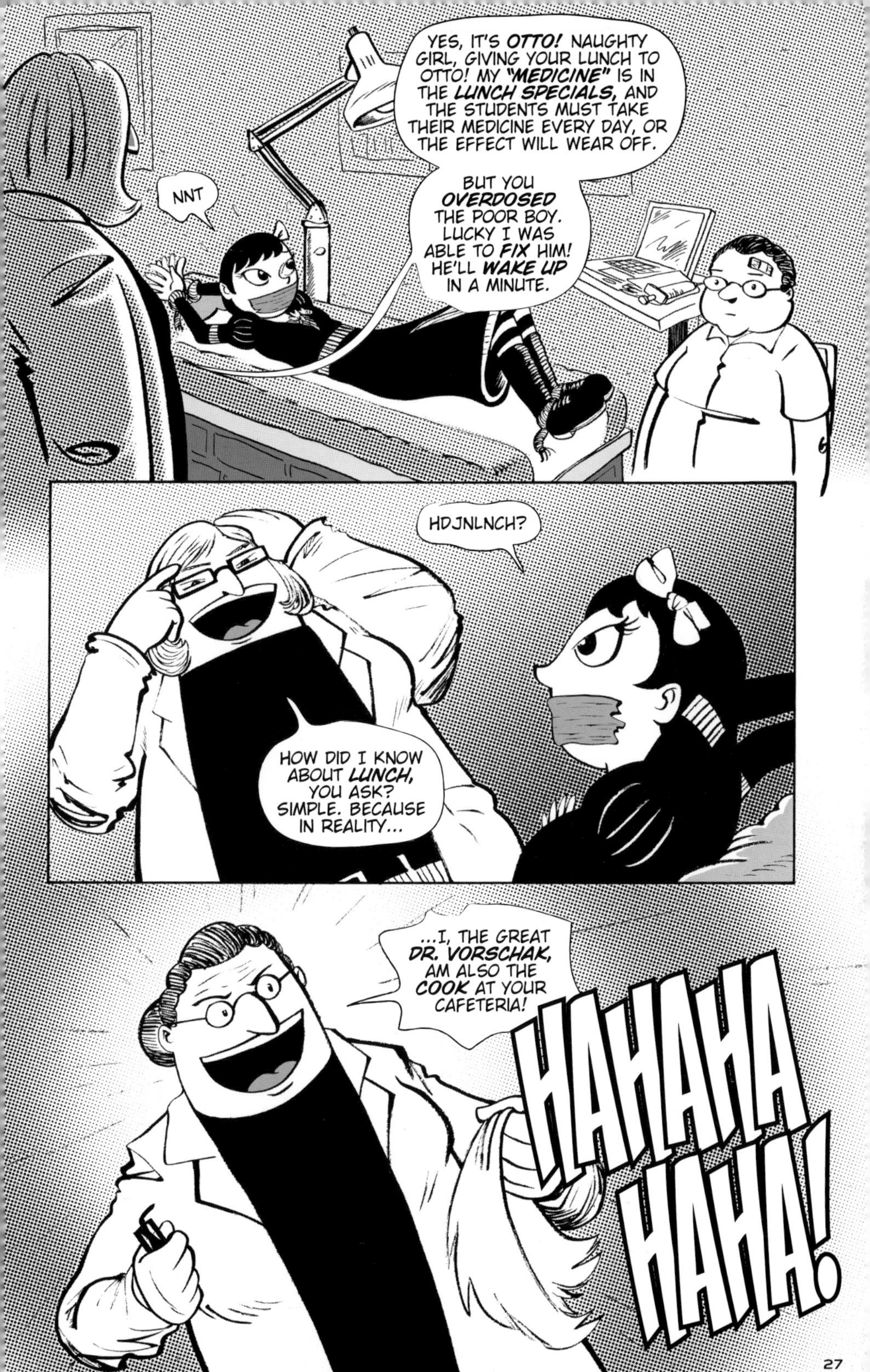
YES, IT'S *OTTO!* NAUGHTY GIRL, GIVING YOUR LUNCH TO OTTO! MY ***"MEDICINE"*** IS IN THE ***LUNCH SPECIALS,*** AND THE STUDENTS MUST TAKE THEIR MEDICINE EVERY DAY, OR THE EFFECT WILL WEAR OFF.
NNT
BUT YOU ***OVERDOSED*** THE POOR BOY. LUCKY I WAS ABLE TO ***FIX*** HIM! HE'LL ***WAKE UP*** IN A MINUTE.
HDJNLNCH?
HOW DID I KNOW ABOUT ***LUNCH,*** YOU ASK? SIMPLE. BECAUSE IN REALITY...
...I, THE GREAT ***DR. VORSCHAK,*** AM ALSO THE ***COOK*** AT YOUR CAFETERIA!
HAHAHA HAHA!

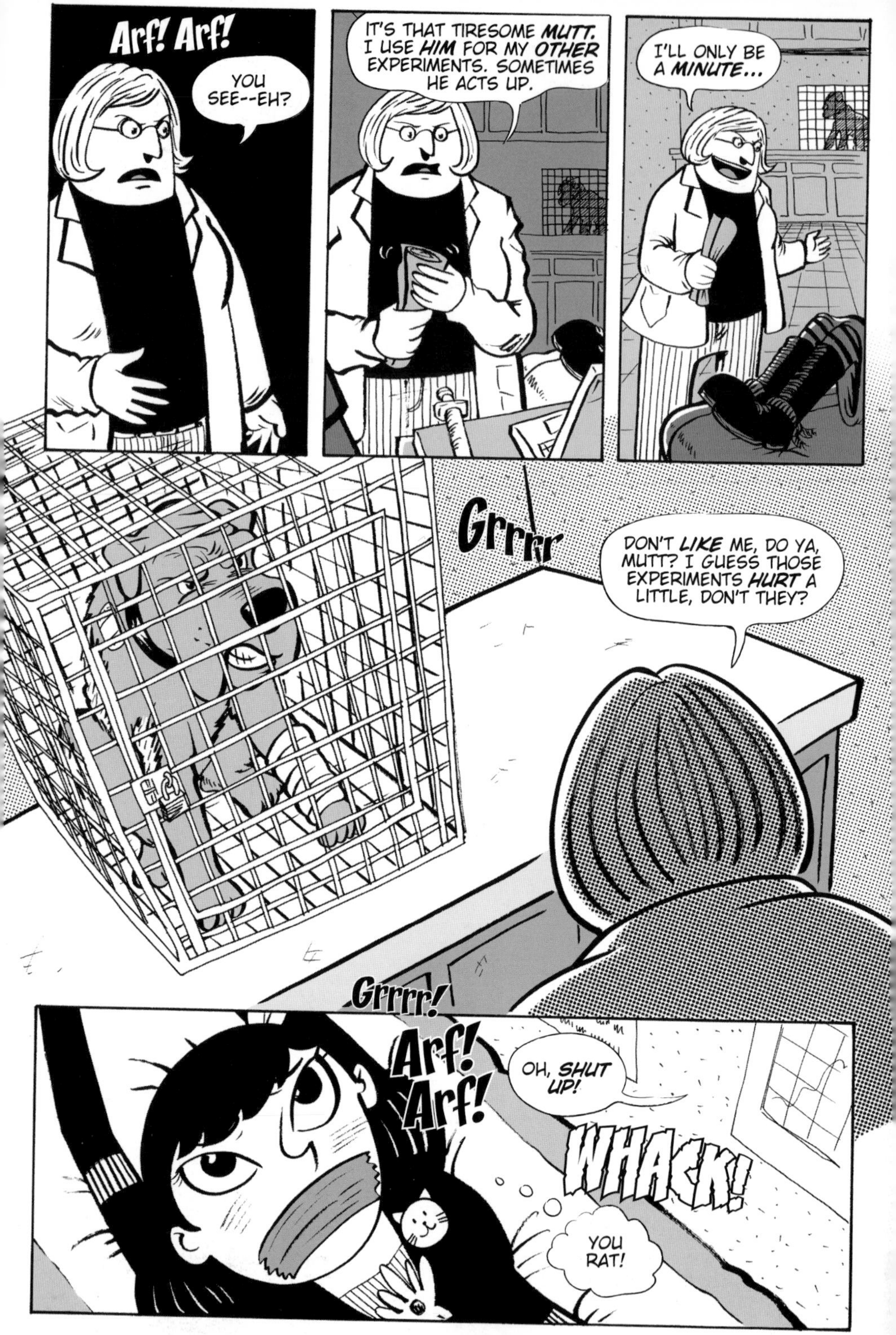
Arf! Arf!
YOU SEE--EH?
IT'S THAT TIRESOME MUTT. I USE HIM FOR MY OTHER EXPERIMENTS. SOMETIMES HE ACTS UP.
I'LL ONLY BE A MINUTE...
Grrrr
DON'T LIKE ME, DO YA, MUTT? I GUESS THOSE EXPERIMENTS HURT A LITTLE, DON'T THEY?
Grrrr!
Arf! Arf!
OH, SHUT UP!
WHACK!
YOU RAT!

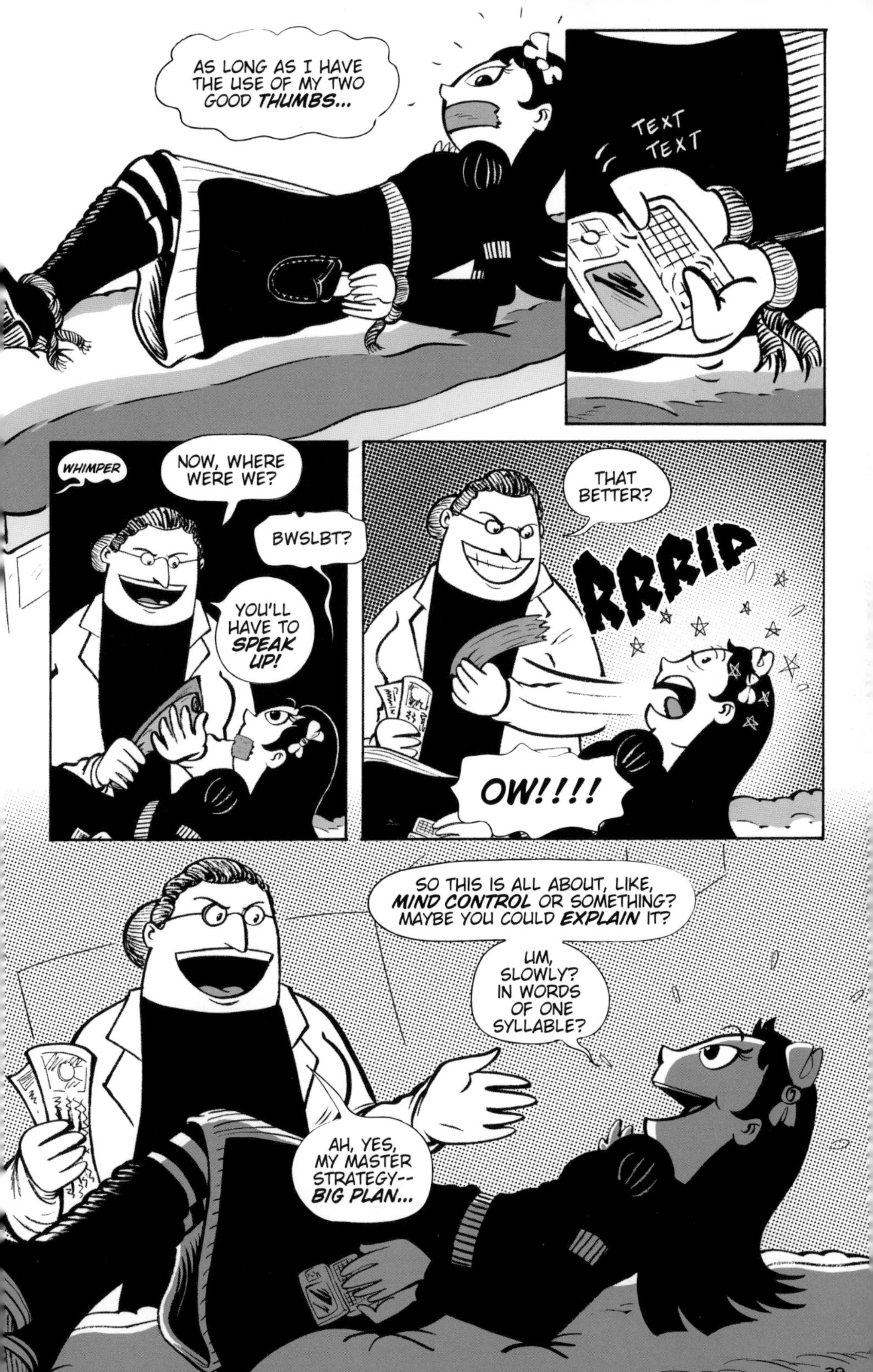
AS LONG AS I HAVE THE USE OF MY TWO GOOD THUMBS...
TEXT TEXT
WHIMPER
NOW, WHERE WERE WE?
BWSLBT?
YOU'LL HAVE TO SPEAK UP!
THAT BETTER?
RRRIP
OW!!!!
SO THIS IS ALL ABOUT, LIKE, MIND CONTROL OR SOMETHING? MAYBE YOU COULD EXPLAIN IT?
UM, SLOWLY? IN WORDS OF ONE SYLLABLE?
AH, YES, MY MASTER STRATEGY--BIG PLAN...

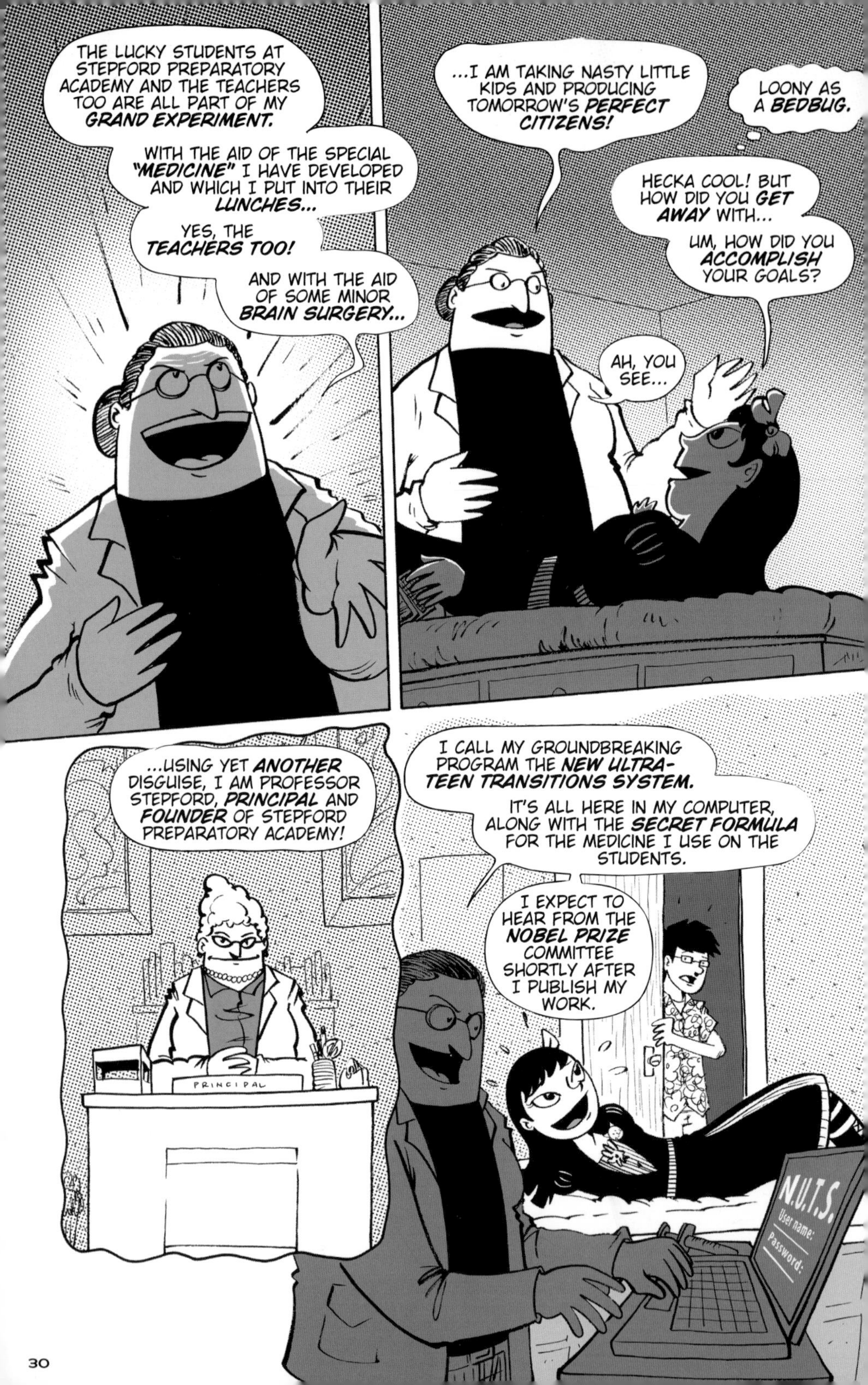
THE LUCKY STUDENTS AT STEPFORD PREPARATORY ACADEMY AND THE TEACHERS TOO ARE ALL PART OF MY GRAND EXPERIMENT.
WITH THE AID OF THE SPECIAL "MEDICINE" I HAVE DEVELOPED AND WHICH I PUT INTO THEIR LUNCHES...
YES, THE TEACHERS TOO!
AND WITH THE AID OF SOME MINOR BRAIN SURGERY...
...I AM TAKING NASTY LITTLE KIDS AND PRODUCING TOMORROW'S PERFECT CITIZENS!
LOONY AS A BEDBUG.
HECKA COOL! BUT HOW DID YOU GET AWAY WITH...
UM, HOW DID YOU ACCOMPLISH YOUR GOALS?
AH, YOU SEE...
...USING YET ANOTHER DISGUISE, I AM PROFESSOR STEPFORD, PRINCIPAL AND FOUNDER OF STEPFORD PREPARATORY ACADEMY!
PRINCIPAL
I CALL MY GROUNDBREAKING PROGRAM THE NEW ULTRA-TEEN TRANSITIONS SYSTEM.
IT'S ALL HERE IN MY COMPUTER, ALONG WITH THE SECRET FORMULA FOR THE MEDICINE I USE ON THE STUDENTS.
I EXPECT TO HEAR FROM THE NOBEL PRIZE COMMITTEE SHORTLY AFTER I PUBLISH MY WORK.
N.U.T.S.
User name:
Password:

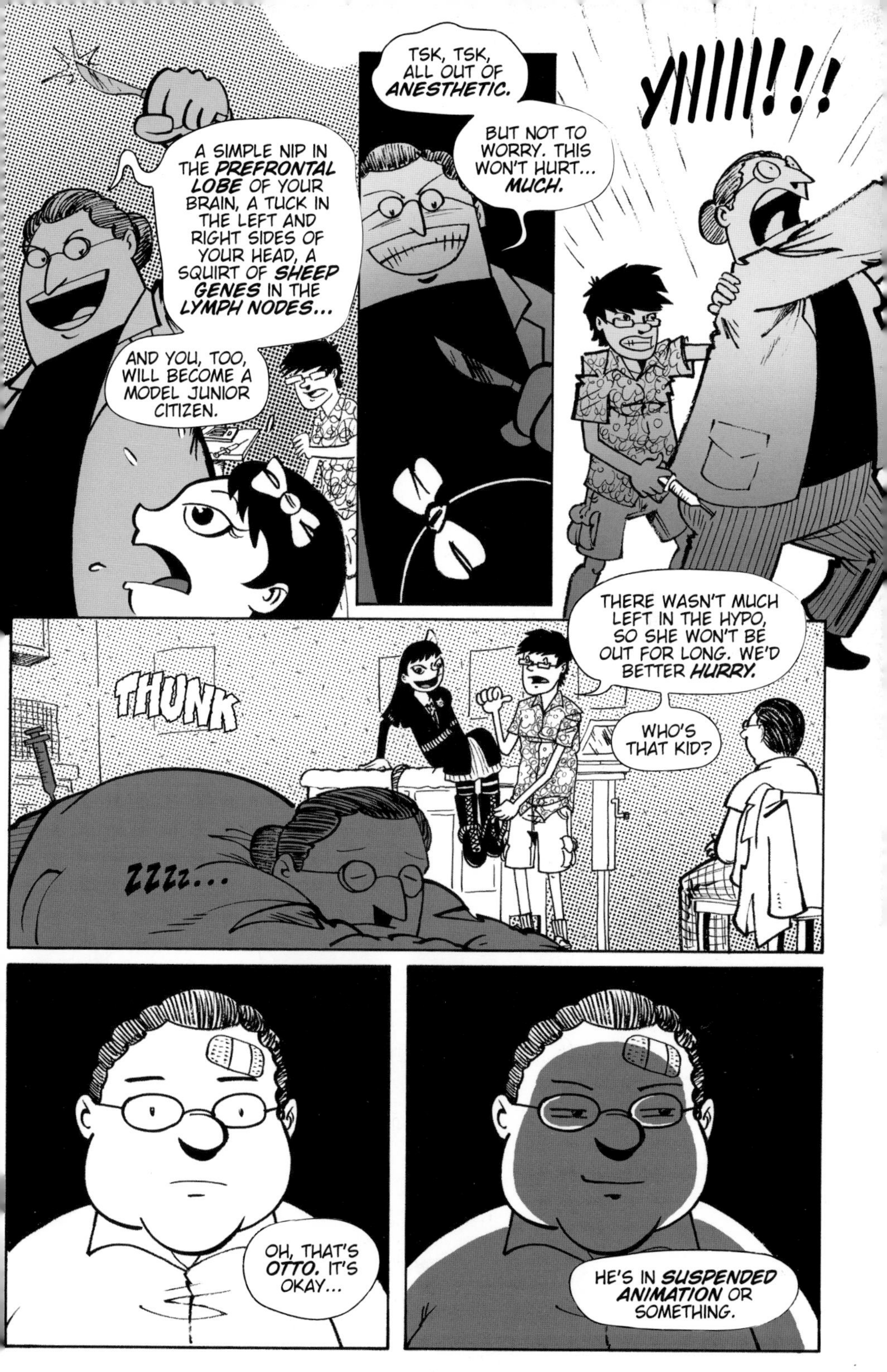
A SIMPLE NIP IN THE PREFRONTAL LOBE OF YOUR BRAIN, A TUCK IN THE LEFT AND RIGHT SIDES OF YOUR HEAD, A SQUIRT OF SHEEP GENES IN THE LYMPH NODES...
AND YOU, TOO, WILL BECOME A MODEL JUNIOR CITIZEN.
TSK, TSK, ALL OUT OF ANESTHETIC.
BUT NOT TO WORRY. THIS WON'T HURT... MUCH.
YIIIIII!!!
THUNK
ZZZz...
THERE WASN'T MUCH LEFT IN THE HYPO, SO SHE WON'T BE OUT FOR LONG. WE'D BETTER HURRY.
WHO'S THAT KID?
OH, THAT'S OTTO. IT'S OKAY...
HE'S IN SUSPENDED ANIMATION OR SOMETHING.

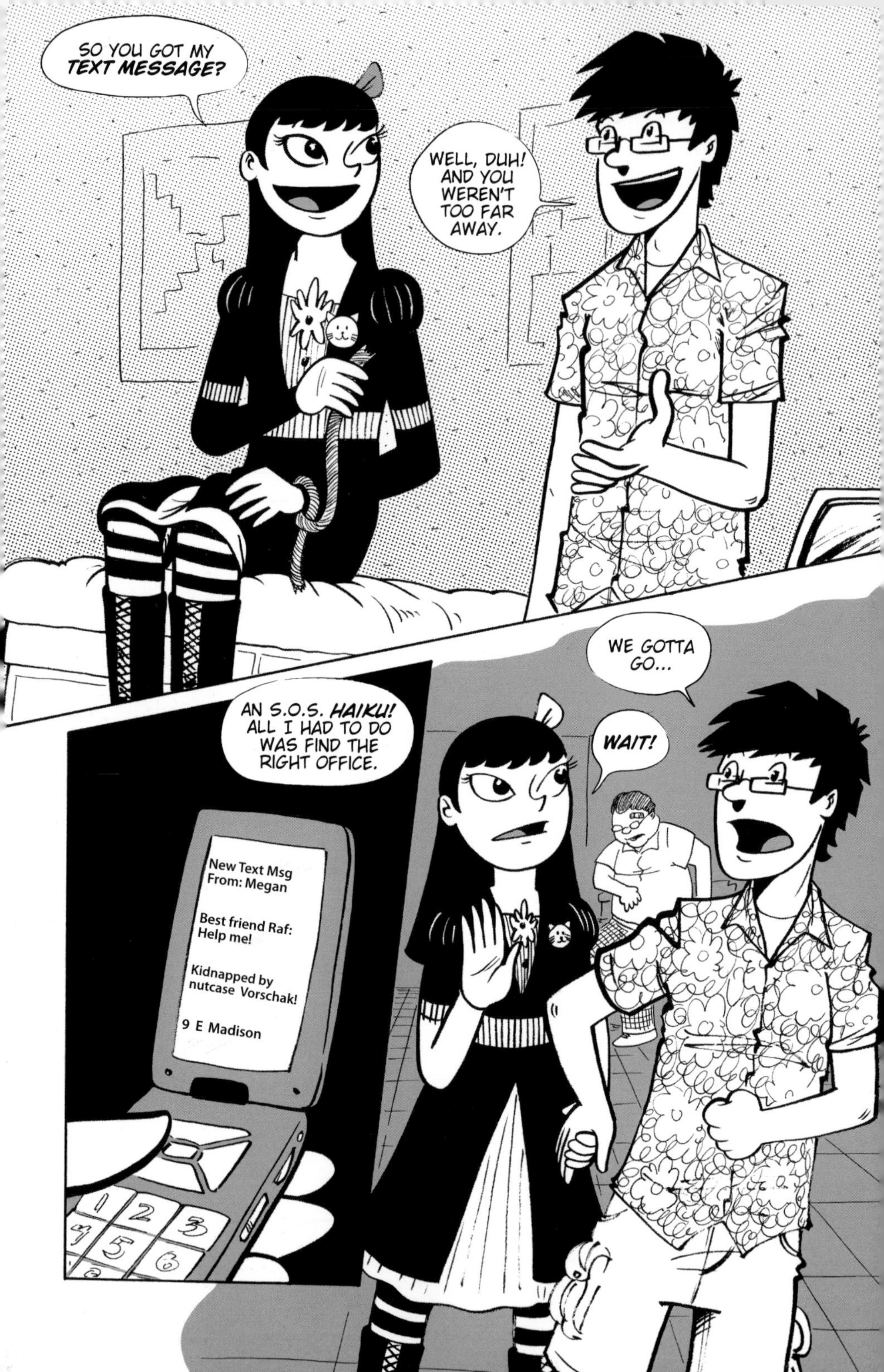
SO YOU GOT MY TEXT MESSAGE?
WELL, DUH! AND YOU WEREN'T TOO FAR AWAY.
AN S.O.S. HAIKU! ALL I HAD TO DO WAS FIND THE RIGHT OFFICE.
New Text Msg
From: Megan
Best friend Raf: Help me!
Kidnapped by nutcase Vorschak!
9 E Madison
WE GOTTA GO...
WAIT!

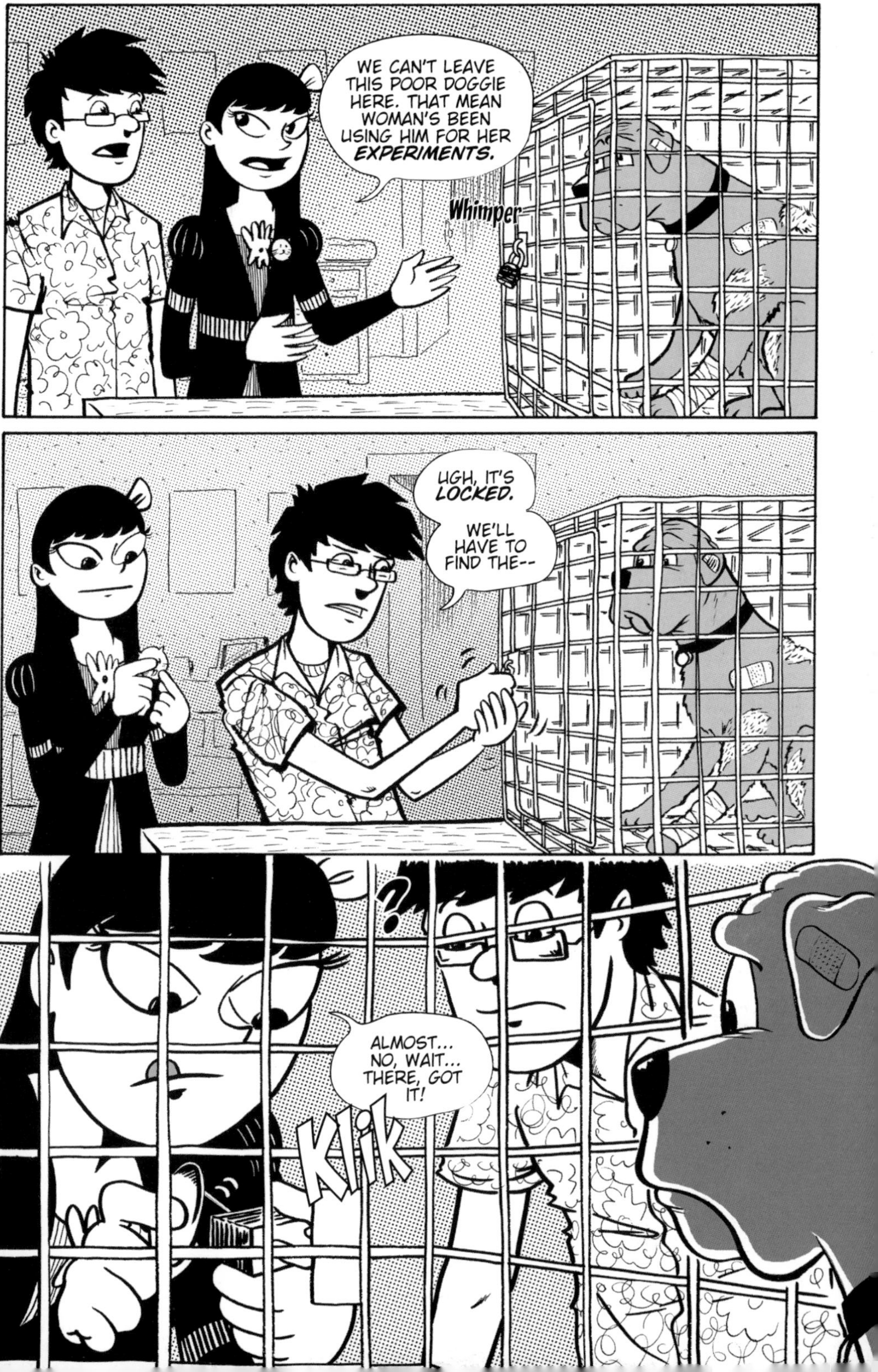
WE CAN'T LEAVE THIS POOR DOGGIE HERE. THAT MEAN WOMAN'S BEEN USING HIM FOR HER EXPERIMENTS.
Whimper
UGH, IT'S LOCKED.
WE'LL HAVE TO FIND THE--
?
ALMOST... NO, WAIT... THERE, GOT IT!
KLIK

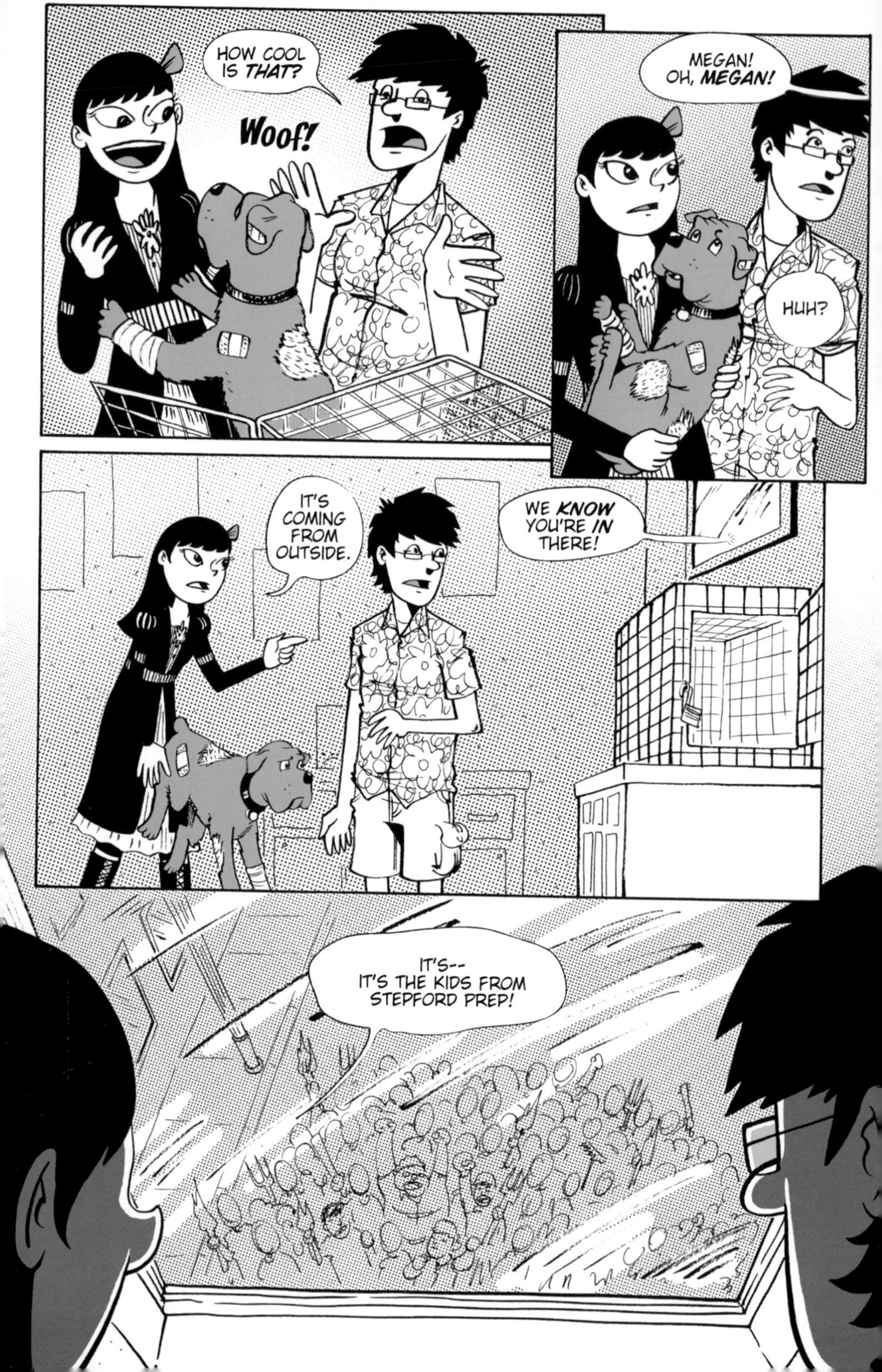
HOW COOL IS THAT?
Woof!
MEGAN! OH, MEGAN!
HUH?
IT'S COMING FROM OUTSIDE.
WE KNOW YOU'RE IN THERE!
IT'S-- IT'S THE KIDS FROM STEPFORD PREP!

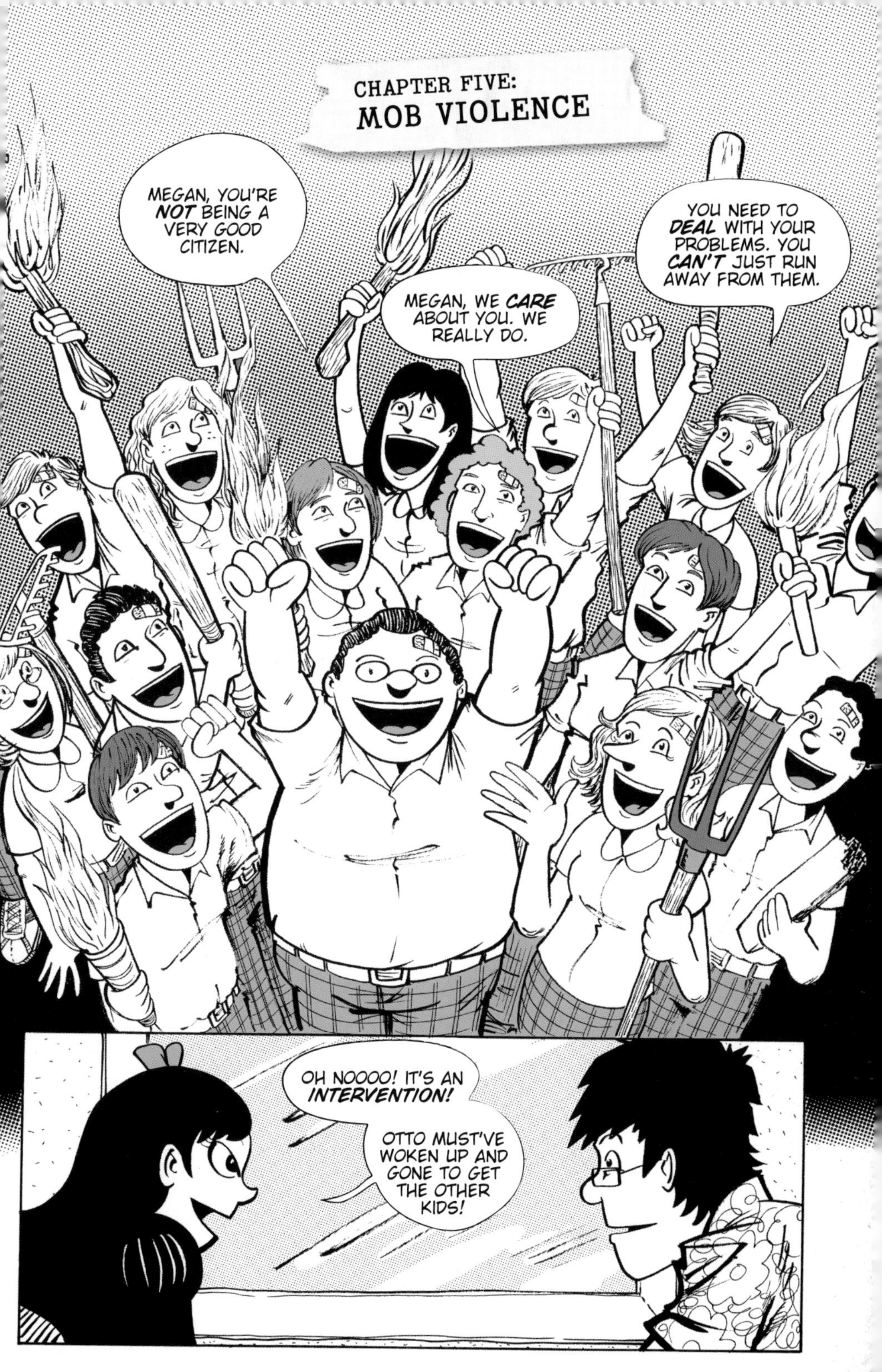
CHAPTER FIVE:
MOB VIOLENCE
MEGAN, YOU'RE NOT BEING A VERY GOOD CITIZEN.
MEGAN, WE CARE ABOUT YOU. WE REALLY DO.
YOU NEED TO DEAL WITH YOUR PROBLEMS. YOU CAN'T JUST RUN AWAY FROM THEM.
OH NOOOO! IT'S AN INTERVENTION!
OTTO MUST'VE WOKEN UP AND GONE TO GET THE OTHER KIDS!

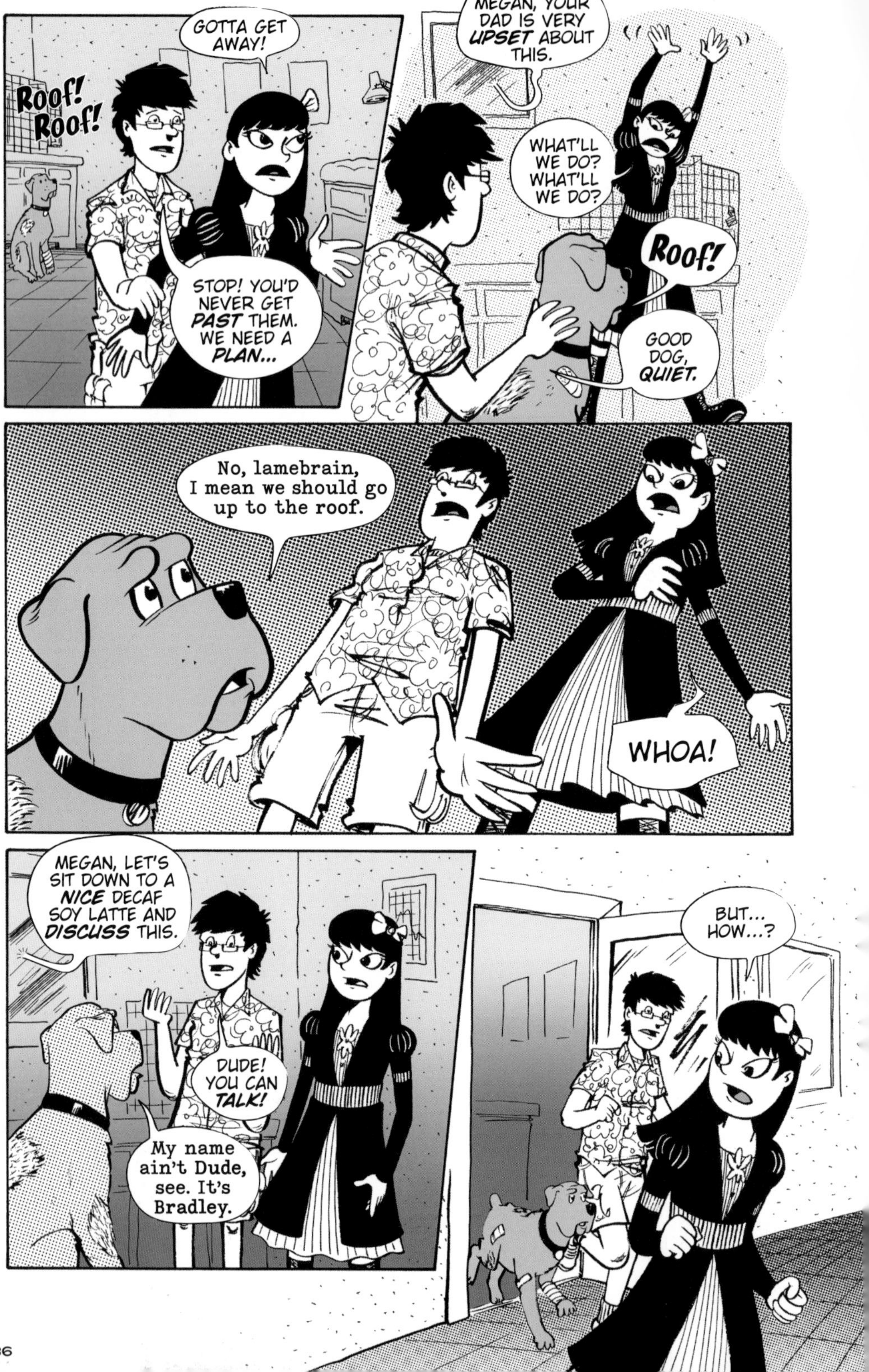
ROOF! ROOF!
GOTTA GET AWAY!
STOP! YOU'D NEVER GET PAST THEM. WE NEED A PLAN...
MEGAN, YOUR DAD IS VERY UPSET ABOUT THIS.
WHAT'LL WE DO? WHAT'LL WE DO?
ROOF!
GOOD DOG, QUIET.
No, lamebrain, I mean we should go up to the roof.
WHOA!
MEGAN, LET'S SIT DOWN TO A NICE DECAF SOY LATTE AND DISCUSS THIS.
DUDE! YOU CAN TALK!
My name ain't Dude, see. It's Bradley.
BUT... HOW...?

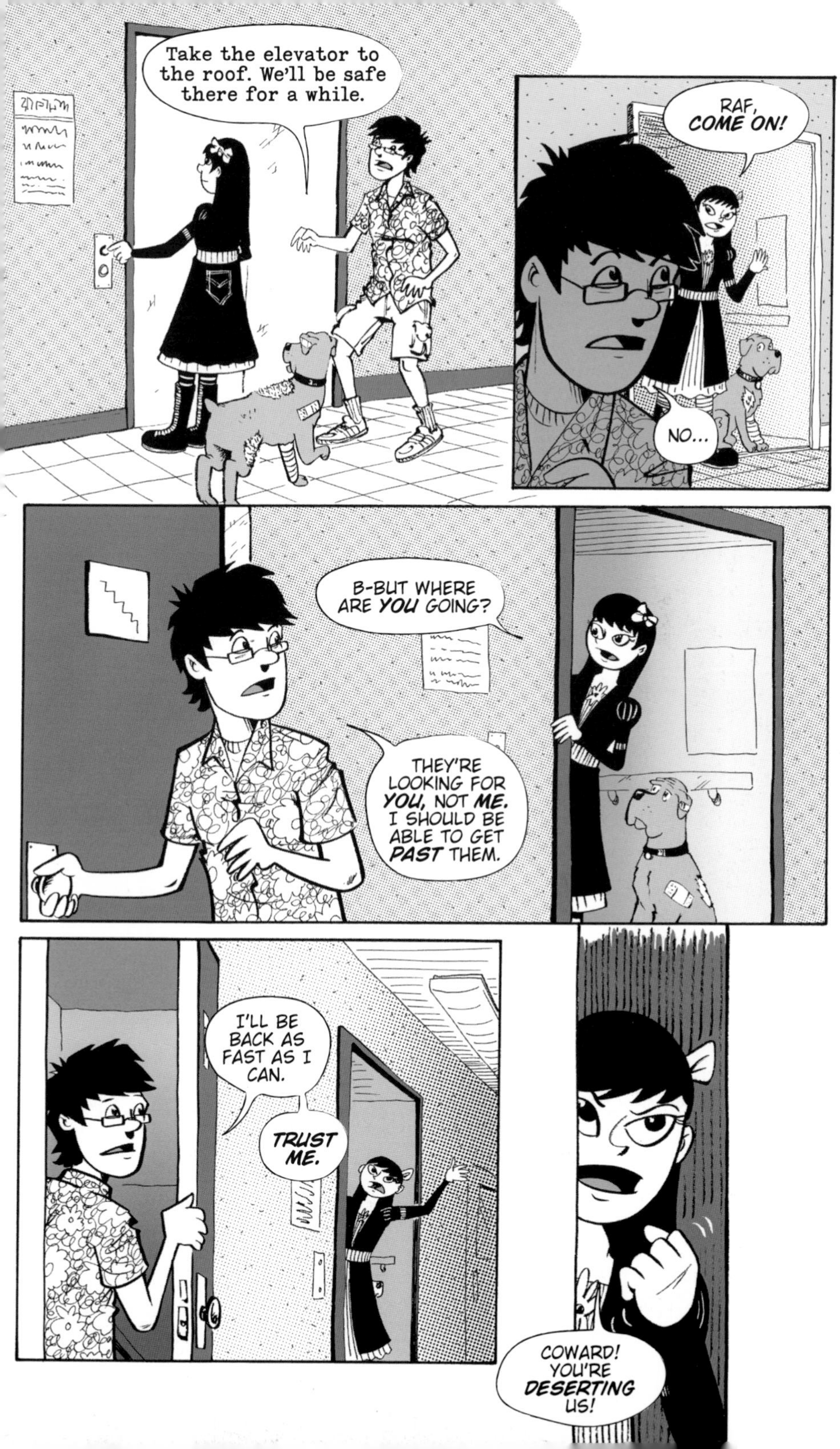
Take the elevator to the roof. We'll be safe there for a while.
RAF, COME ON!
NO...
B-BUT WHERE ARE YOU GOING?
THEY'RE LOOKING FOR YOU, NOT ME. I SHOULD BE ABLE TO GET PAST THEM.
I'LL BE BACK AS FAST AS I CAN.
TRUST ME.
COWARD! YOU'RE DESERTING US!

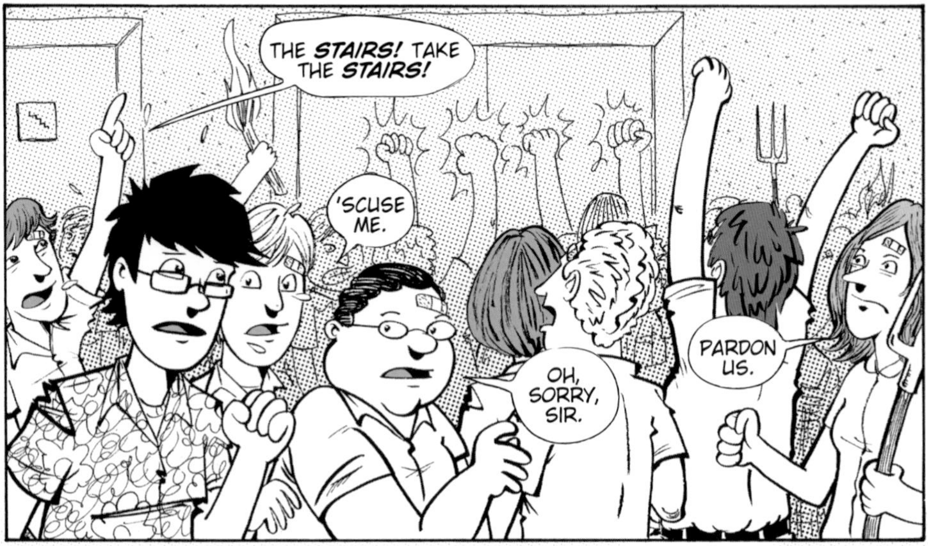
THE STAIRS! TAKE THE STAIRS!
'SCUSE ME.
OH, SORRY, SIR.
PARDON US.

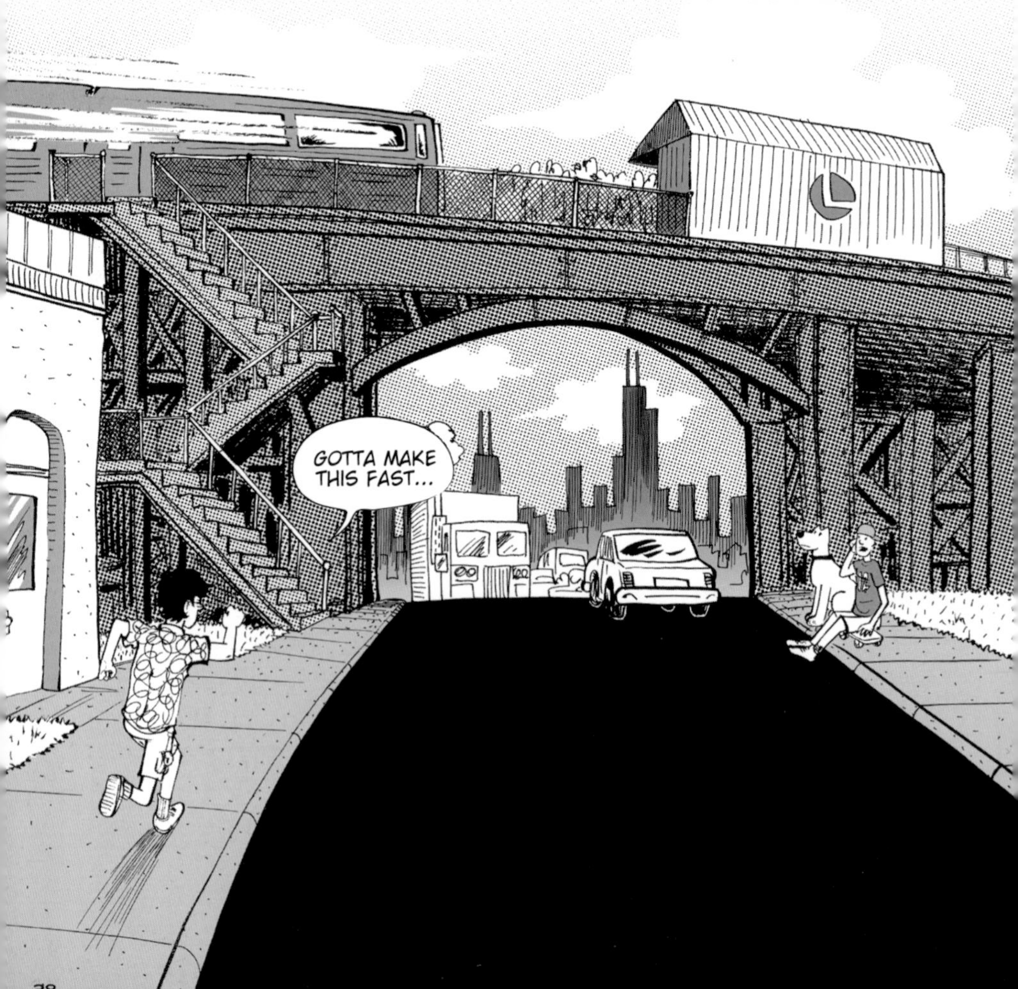
GOTTA MAKE THIS FAST...

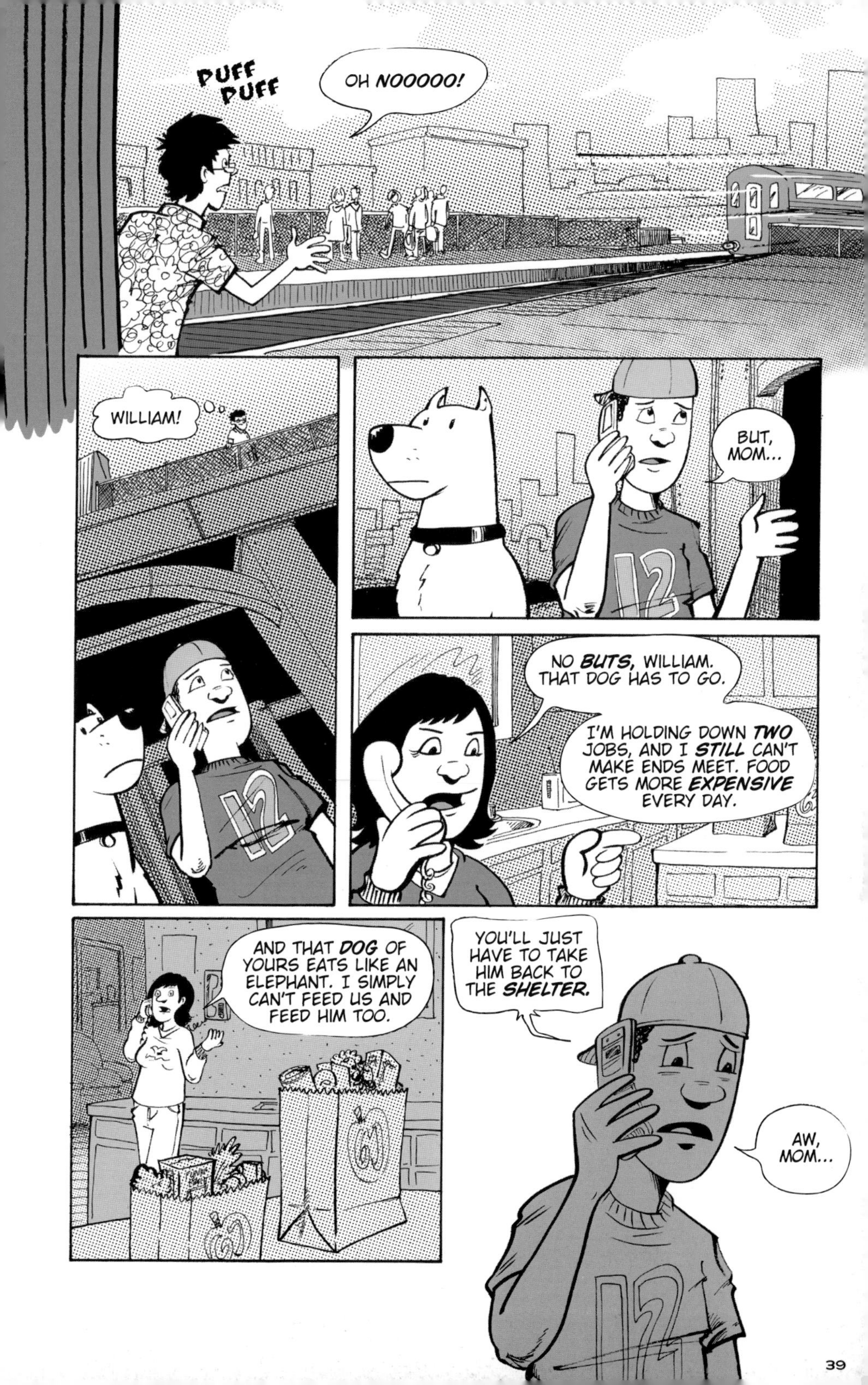
PUFF PUFF
OH NOOOOO!
WILLIAM!
BUT, MOM...
NO BUTS, WILLIAM. THAT DOG HAS TO GO.
I'M HOLDING DOWN TWO JOBS, AND I STILL CAN'T MAKE ENDS MEET. FOOD GETS MORE EXPENSIVE EVERY DAY.
AND THAT DOG OF YOURS EATS LIKE AN ELEPHANT. I SIMPLY CAN'T FEED US AND FEED HIM TOO.
YOU'LL JUST HAVE TO TAKE HIM BACK TO THE SHELTER.
AW, MOM...

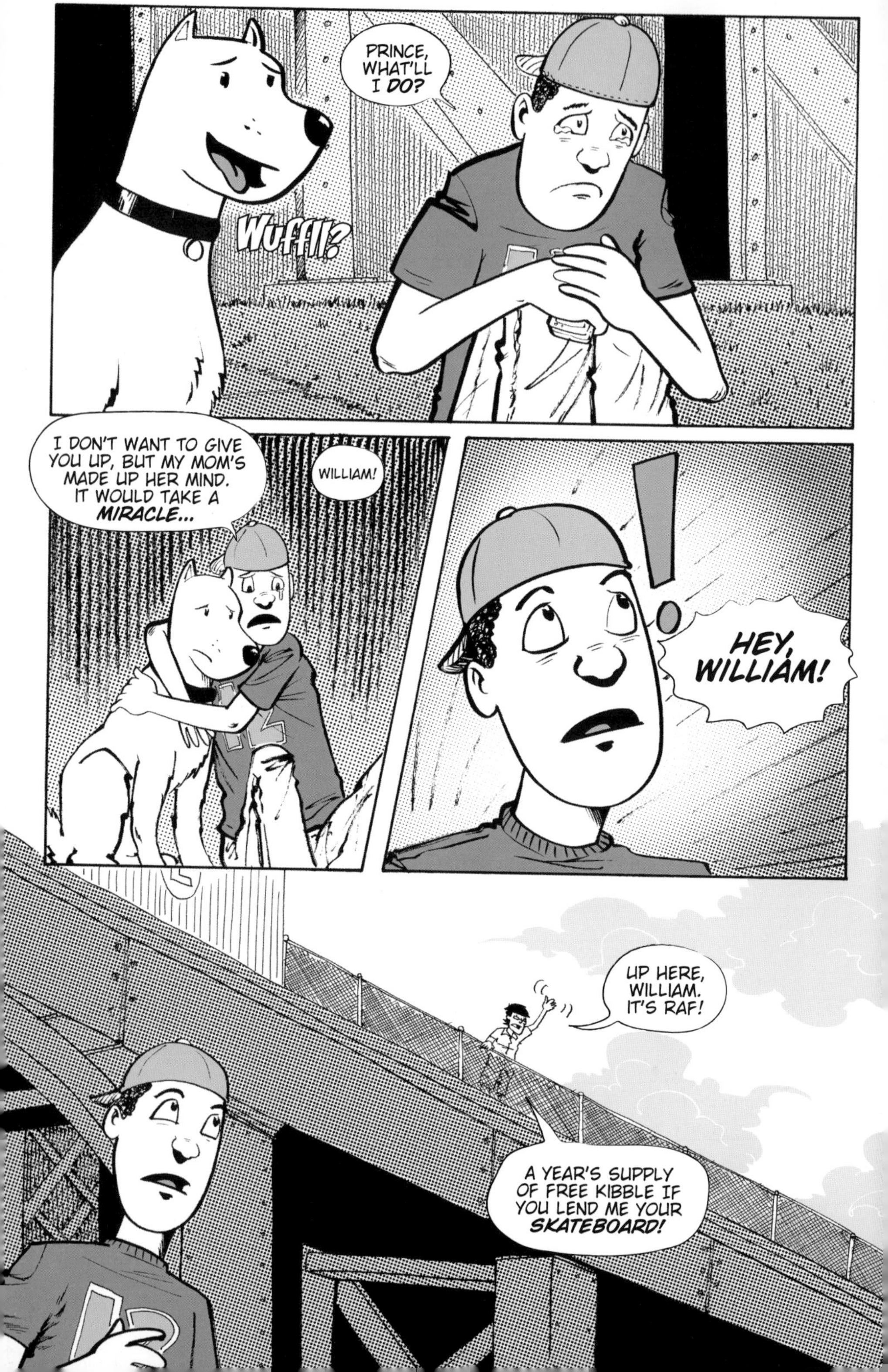

PRINCE, WHAT'LL I DO?
WUFF!?
I DON'T WANT TO GIVE YOU UP, BUT MY MOM'S MADE UP HER MIND. IT WOULD TAKE A MIRACLE...
WILLIAM!
HEY, WILLIAM!
UP HERE, WILLIAM. IT'S RAF!
A YEAR'S SUPPLY OF FREE KIBBLE IF YOU LEND ME YOUR SKATEBOARD!

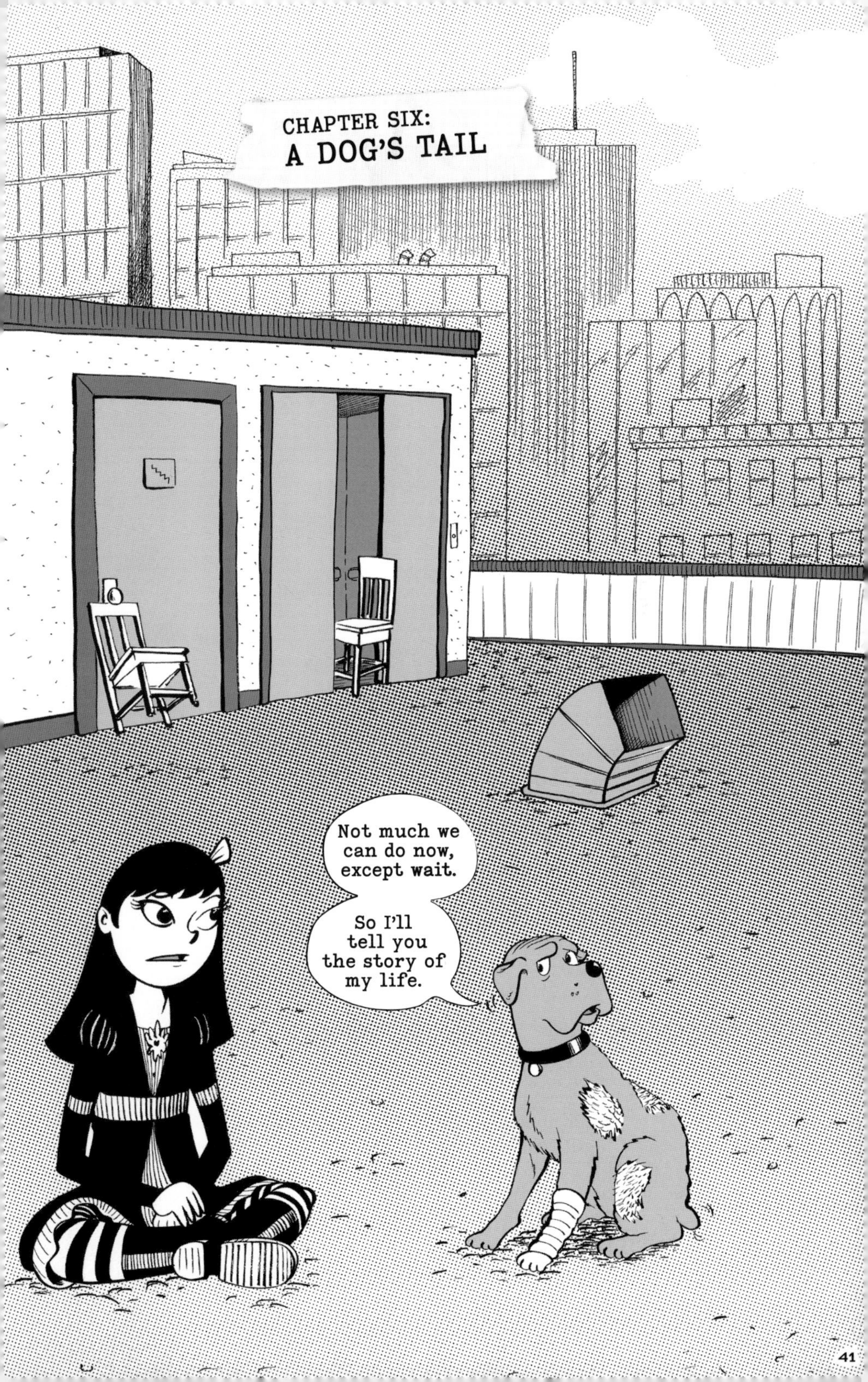

CHAPTER SIX:
A DOG'S TAIL
Not much we can do now, except wait.
So I'll tell you the story of my life.

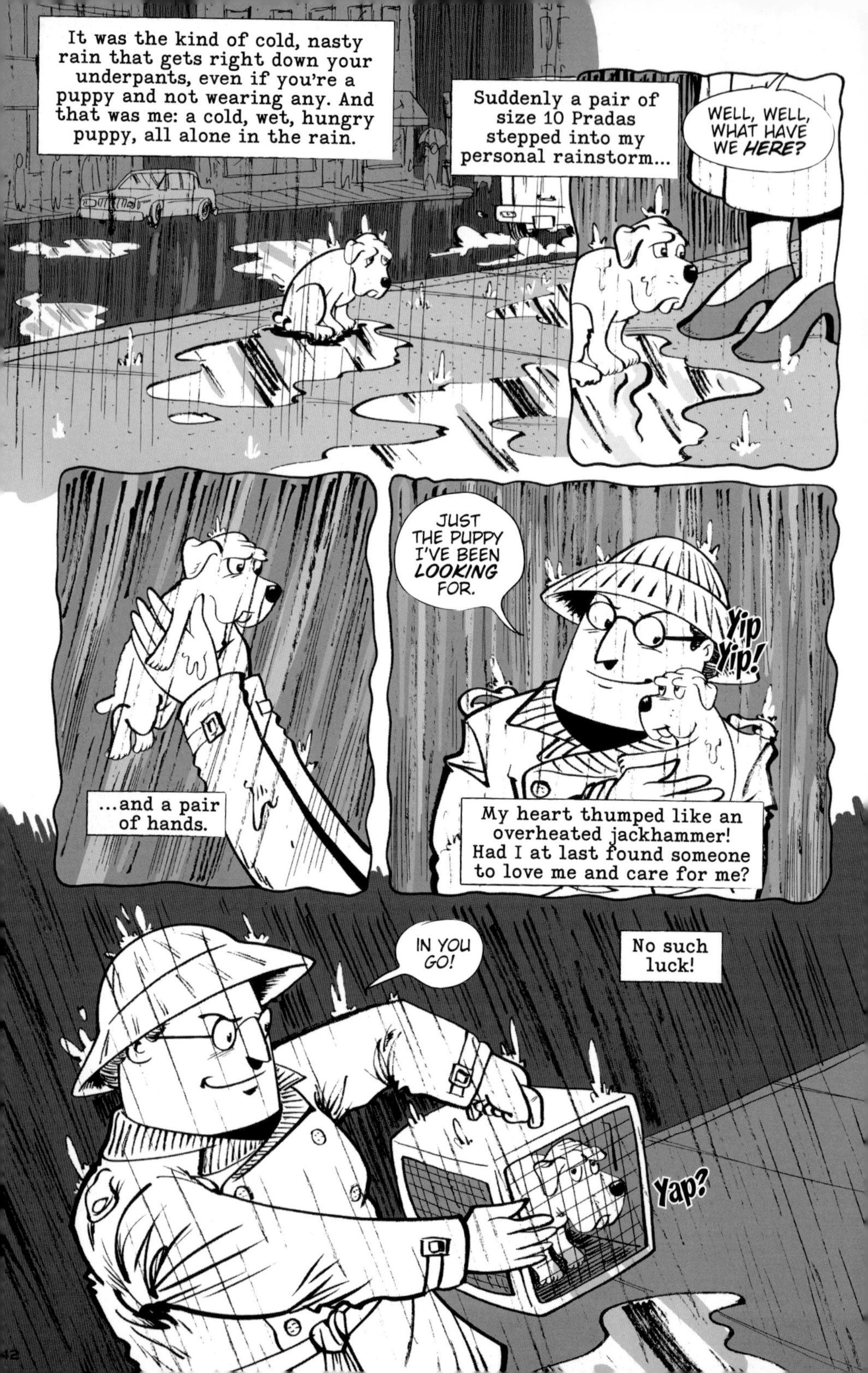
It was the kind of cold, nasty rain that gets right down your underpants, even if you're a puppy and not wearing any. And that was me: a cold, wet, hungry puppy, all alone in the rain.
Suddenly a pair of size 10 Pradas stepped into my personal rainstorm...
WELL, WELL, WHAT HAVE WE HERE?
...and a pair of hands.
JUST THE PUPPY I'VE BEEN LOOKING FOR.
Yip Yip!
My heart thumped like an overheated jackhammer! Had I at last found someone to love me and care for me?
IN YOU GO!
No such luck!
Yap?

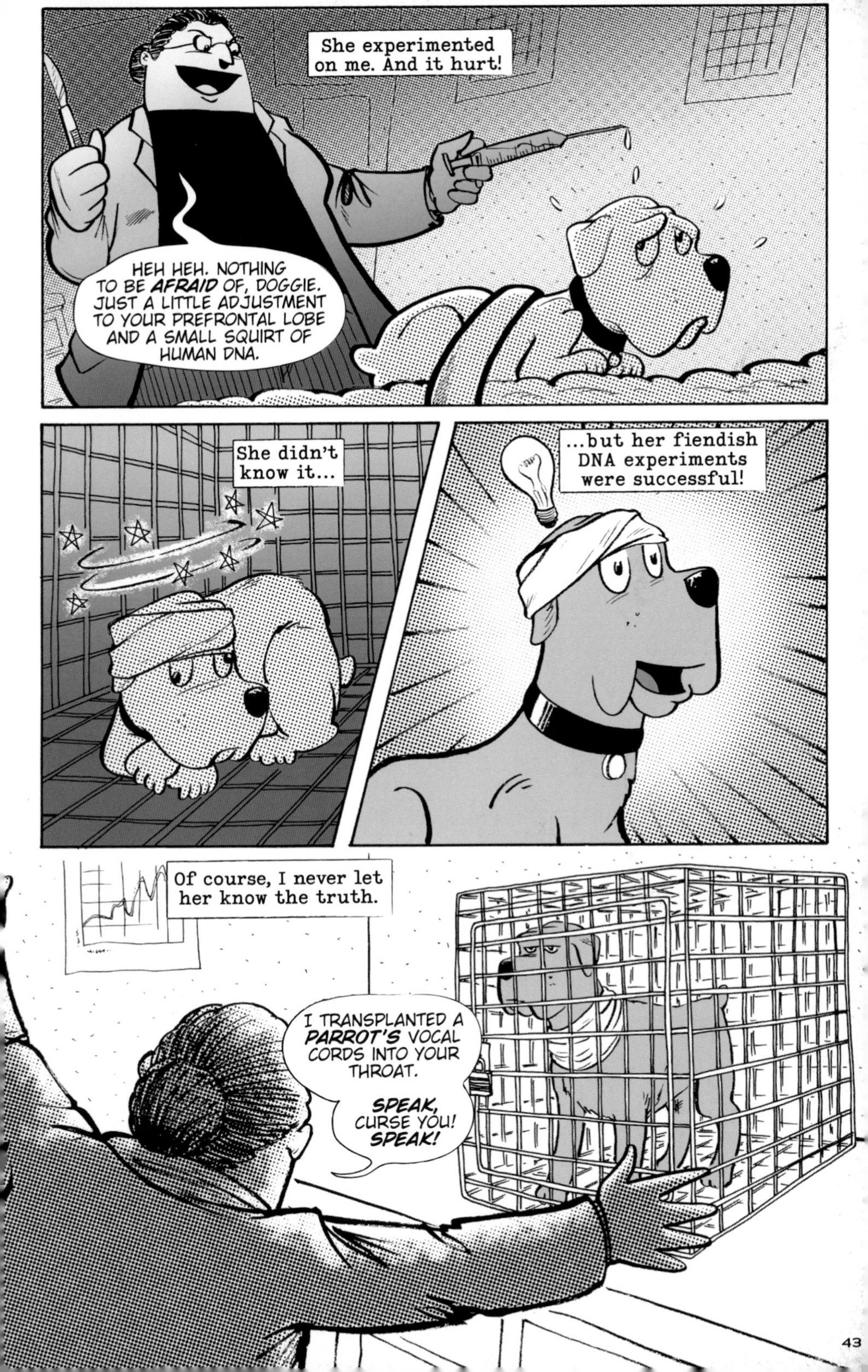
She experimented on me. And it hurt!
HEH HEH. NOTHING TO BE AFRAID OF, DOGGIE. JUST A LITTLE ADJUSTMENT TO YOUR PREFRONTAL LOBE AND A SMALL SQUIRT OF HUMAN DNA.
She didn't know it...
...but her fiendish DNA experiments were successful!
Of course, I never let her know the truth.
I TRANSPLANTED A PARROT'S VOCAL CORDS INTO YOUR THROAT.
SPEAK, CURSE YOU! SPEAK!

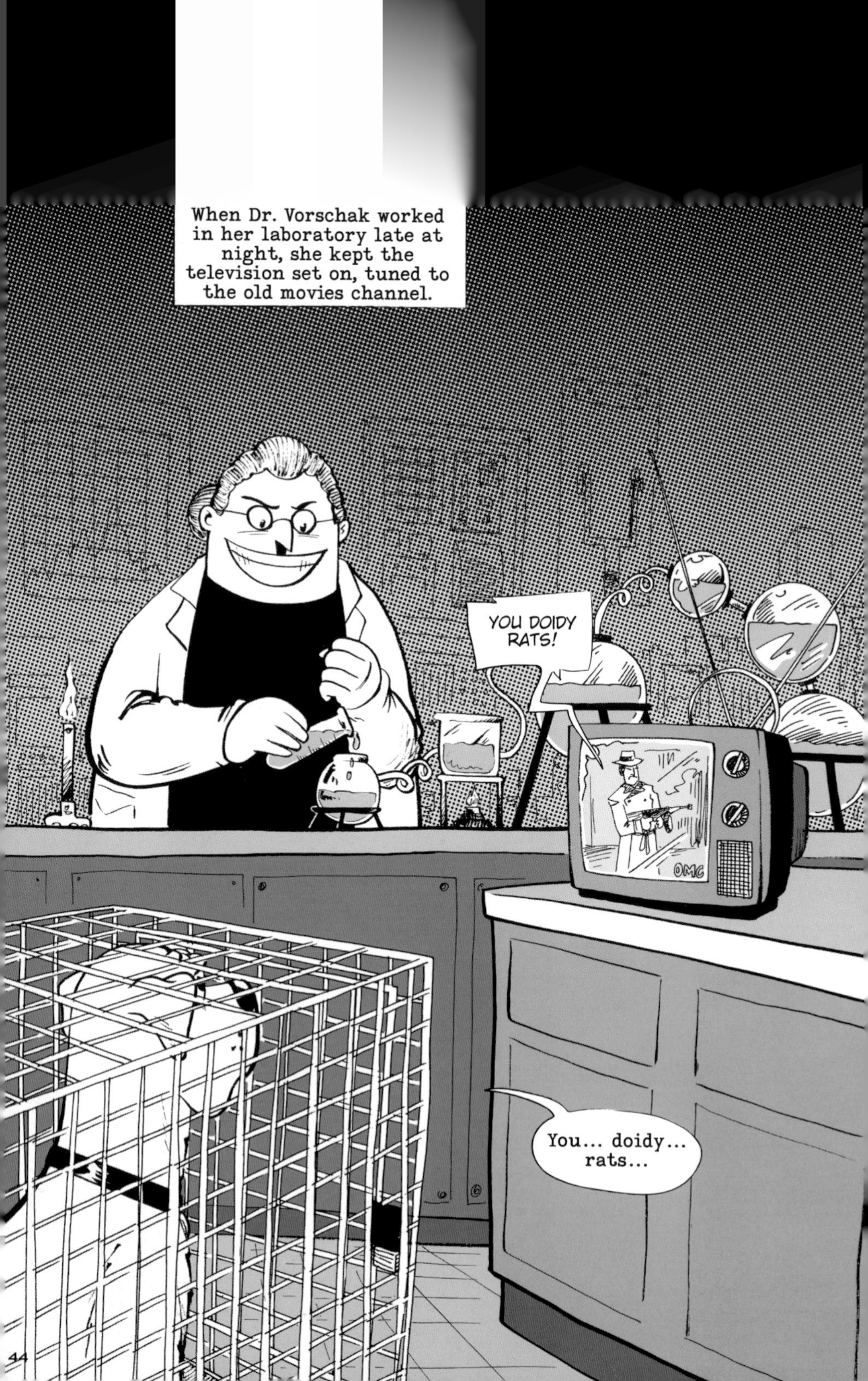

When Dr. Vorschak worked in her laboratory late at night, she kept the television set on, tuned to the old movies channel.
YOU DOIDY RATS!
OMC
You... doidy... rats...

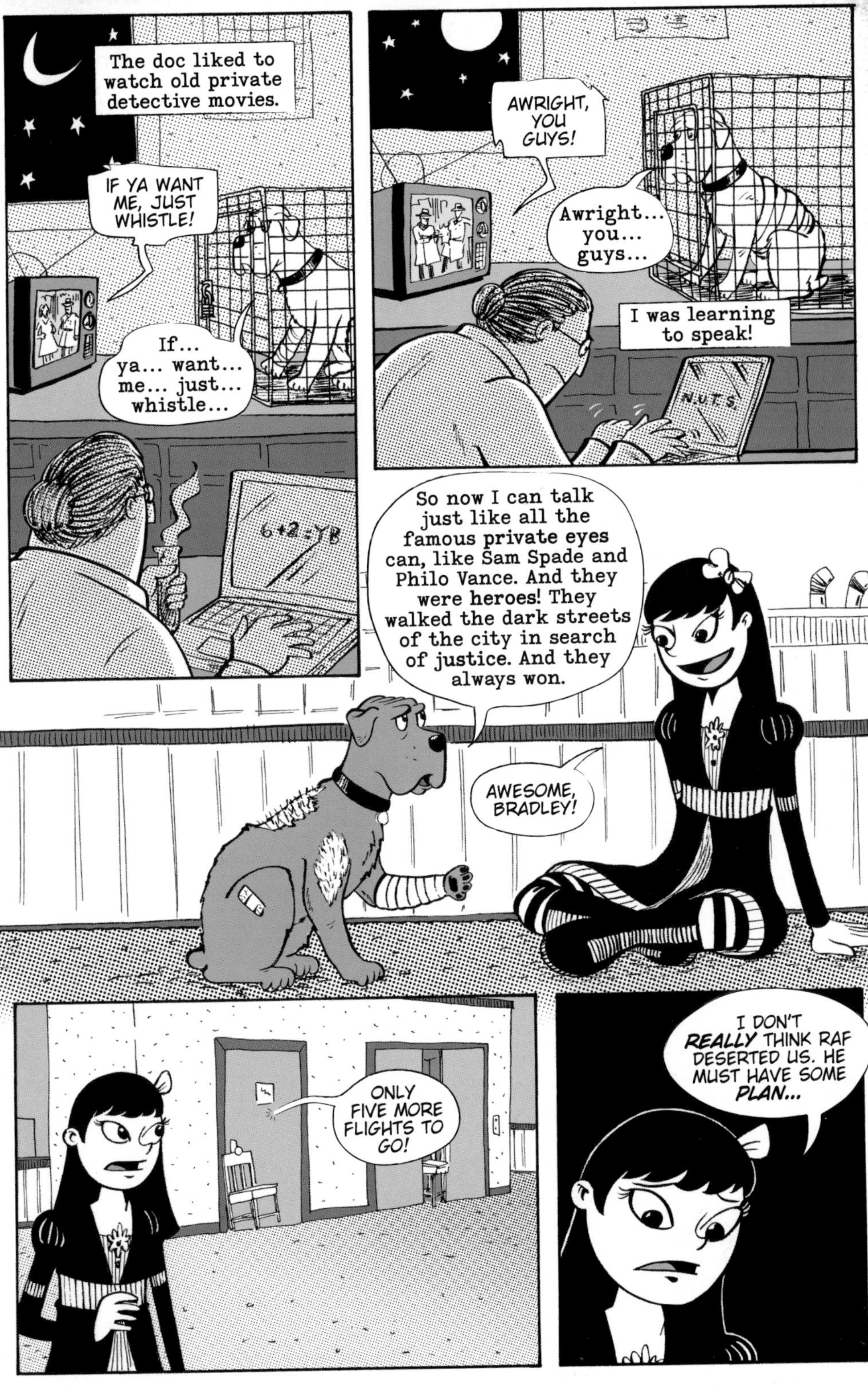

The doc liked to watch old private detective movies.
IF YA WANT ME, JUST WHISTLE!
If... ya... want... me... just... whistle...
6+2=YB
AWRIGHT, YOU GUYS!
Awright... you... guys...
I was learning to speak!
N.U.T.S.
So now I can talk just like all the famous private eyes can, like Sam Spade and Philo Vance. And they were heroes! They walked the dark streets of the city in search of justice. And they always won.
AWESOME, BRADLEY!
ONLY FIVE MORE FLIGHTS TO GO!
I DON'T REALLY THINK RAF DESERTED US. HE MUST HAVE SOME PLAN...

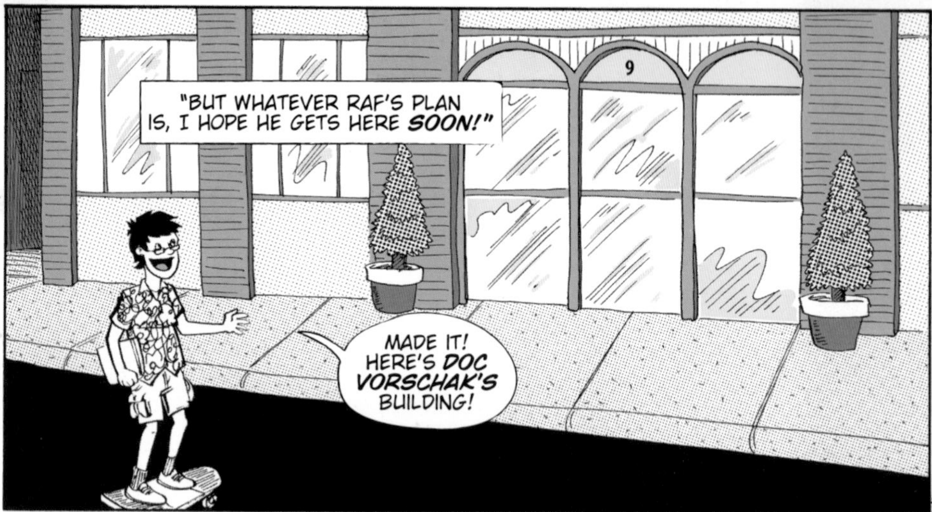
"BUT WHATEVER RAF'S PLAN IS, I HOPE HE GETS HERE SOON!"
MADE IT! HERE'S DOC VORSCHAK'S BUILDING!

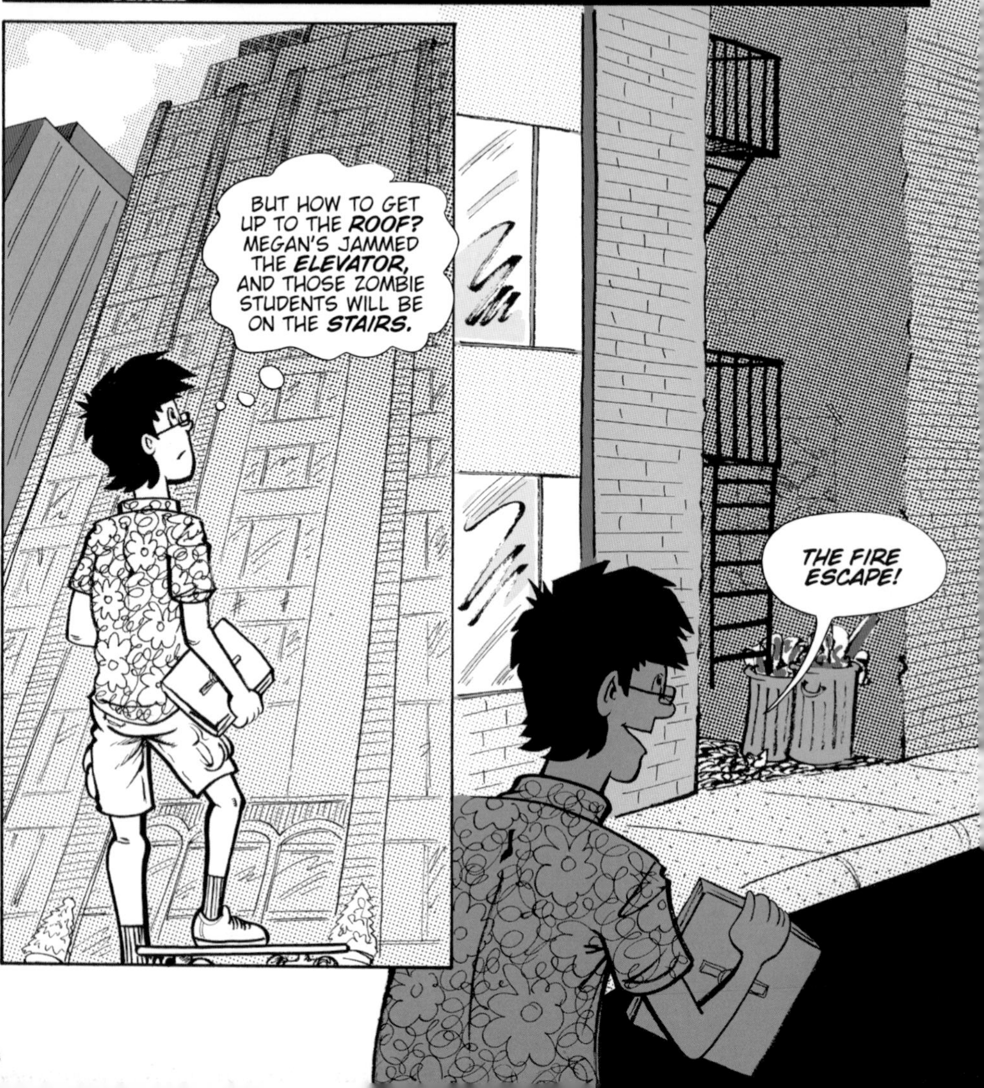
BUT HOW TO GET UP TO THE ROOF? MEGAN'S JAMMED THE ELEVATOR, AND THOSE ZOMBIE STUDENTS WILL BE ON THE STAIRS.
THE FIRE ESCAPE!

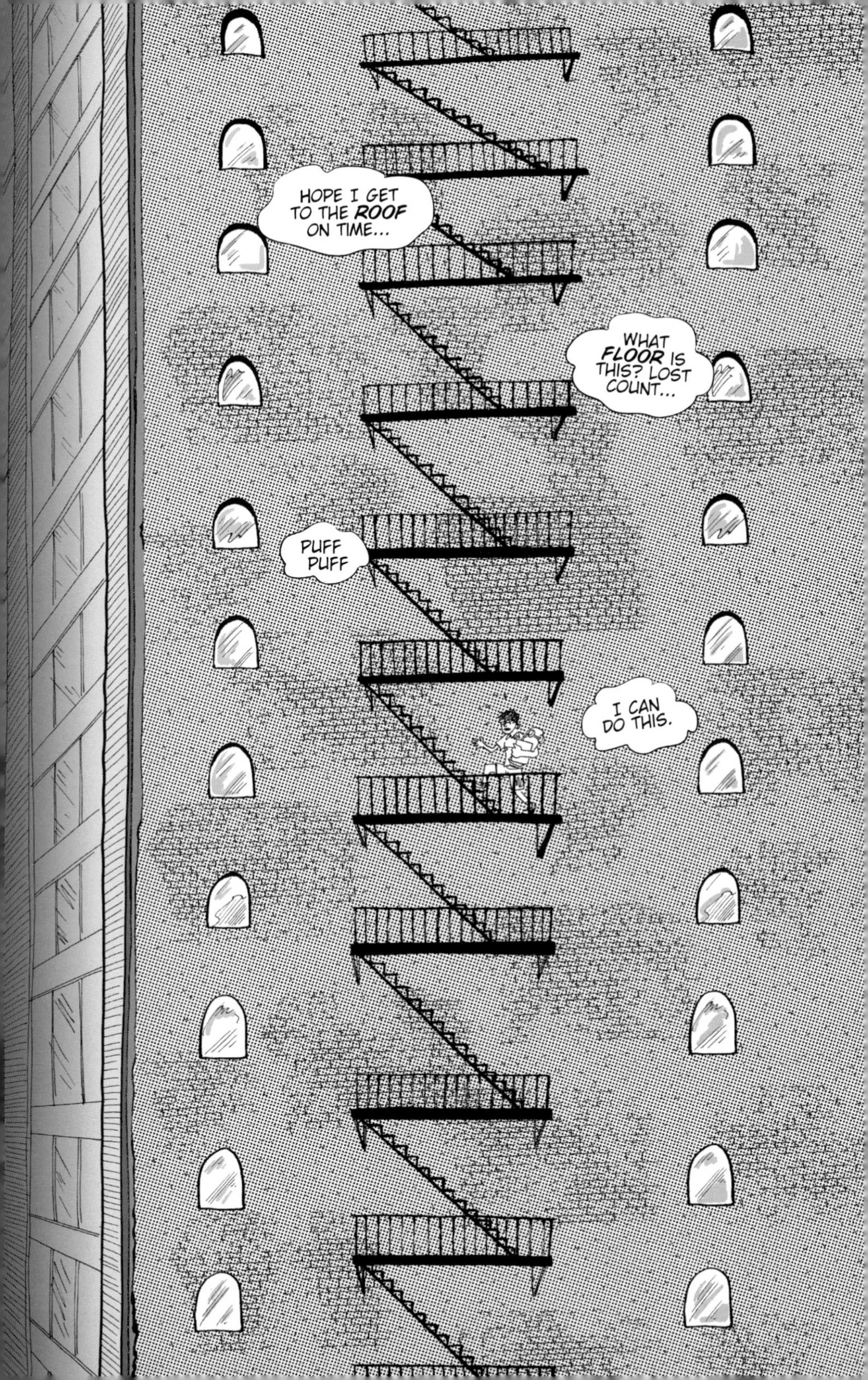
HOPE I GET TO THE ROOF ON TIME...
WHAT FLOOR IS THIS? LOST COUNT...
PUFF PUFF
I CAN DO THIS.

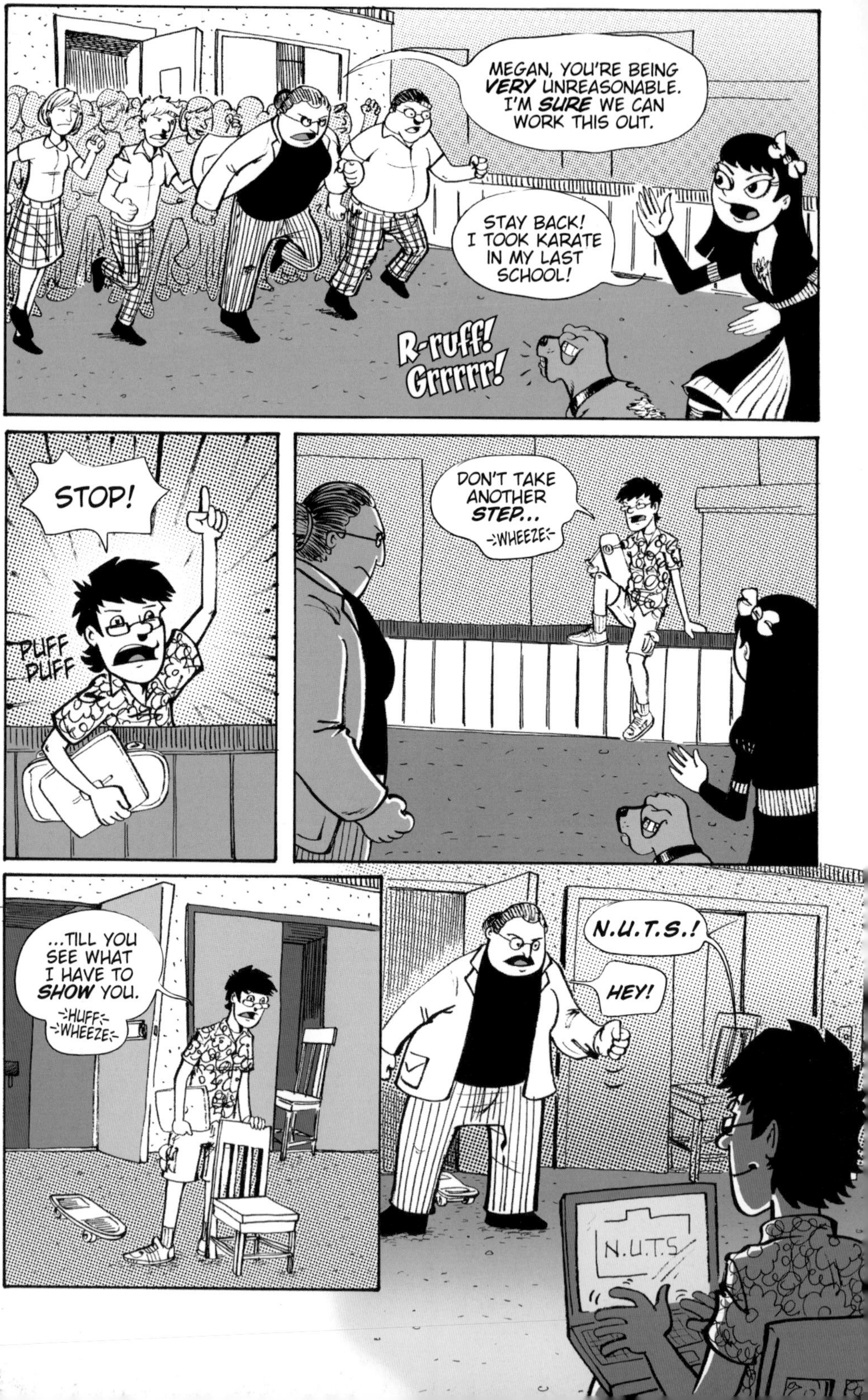
MEGAN, YOU'RE BEING VERY UNREASONABLE. I'M SURE WE CAN WORK THIS OUT.
STAY BACK! I TOOK KARATE IN MY LAST SCHOOL!
R-ruff! Grrrrr!
STOP!
PUFF PUFF
DON'T TAKE ANOTHER STEP...
-WHEEZE-
...TILL YOU SEE WHAT I HAVE TO SHOW YOU.
-HUFF-
-WHEEZE-
N.U.T.S.!
HEY!
N.U.T.S

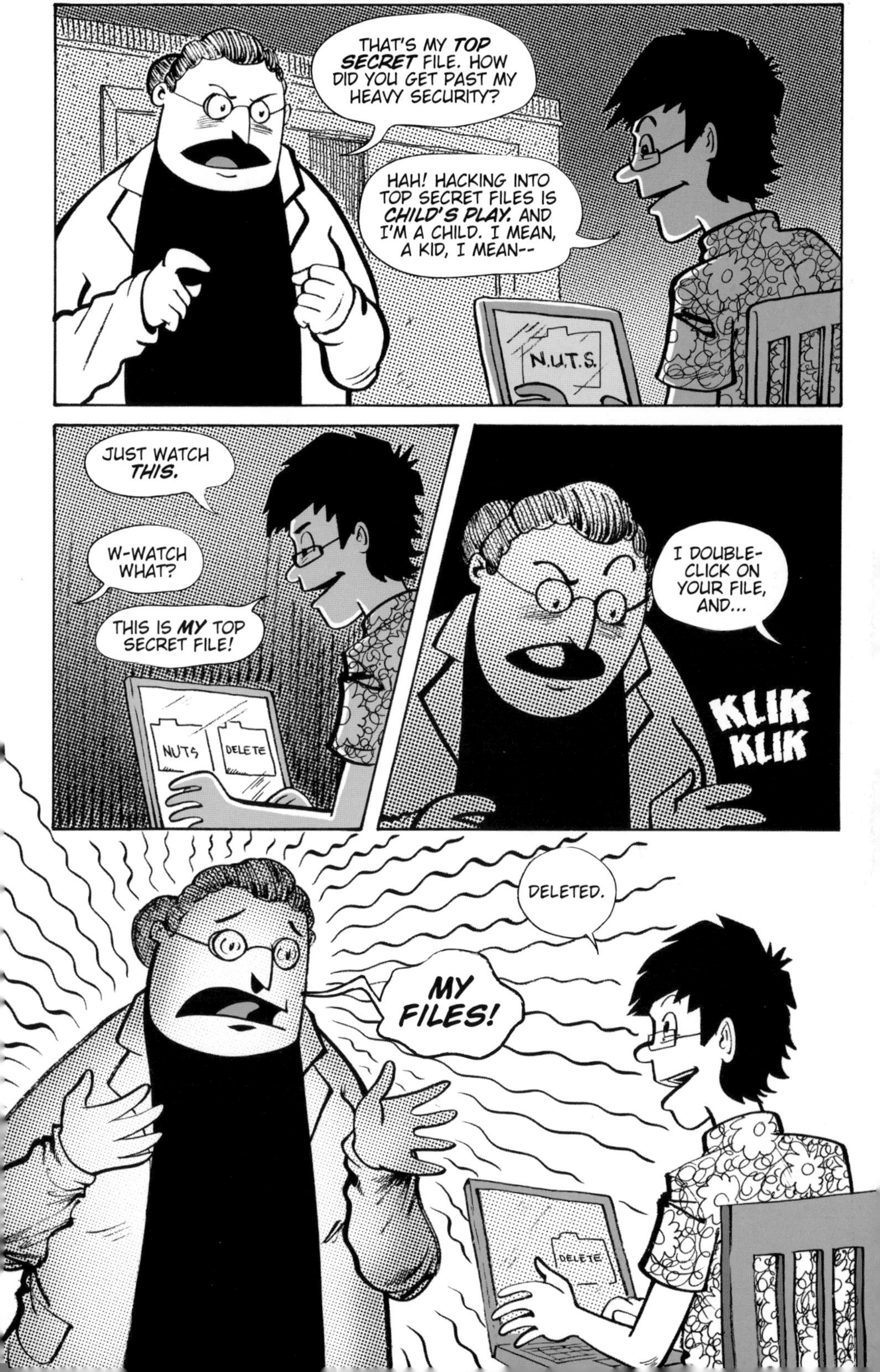
THAT'S MY TOP SECRET FILE. HOW DID YOU GET PAST MY HEAVY SECURITY?
HAH! HACKING INTO TOP SECRET FILES IS CHILD'S PLAY. AND I'M A CHILD. I MEAN, A KID, I MEAN--
N.U.T.S.
JUST WATCH THIS.
W-WATCH WHAT?
THIS IS MY TOP SECRET FILE!
NUTS
DELETE
I DOUBLE-CLICK ON YOUR FILE, AND...
KLIK KLIK
DELETED.
MY FILES!
DELETE

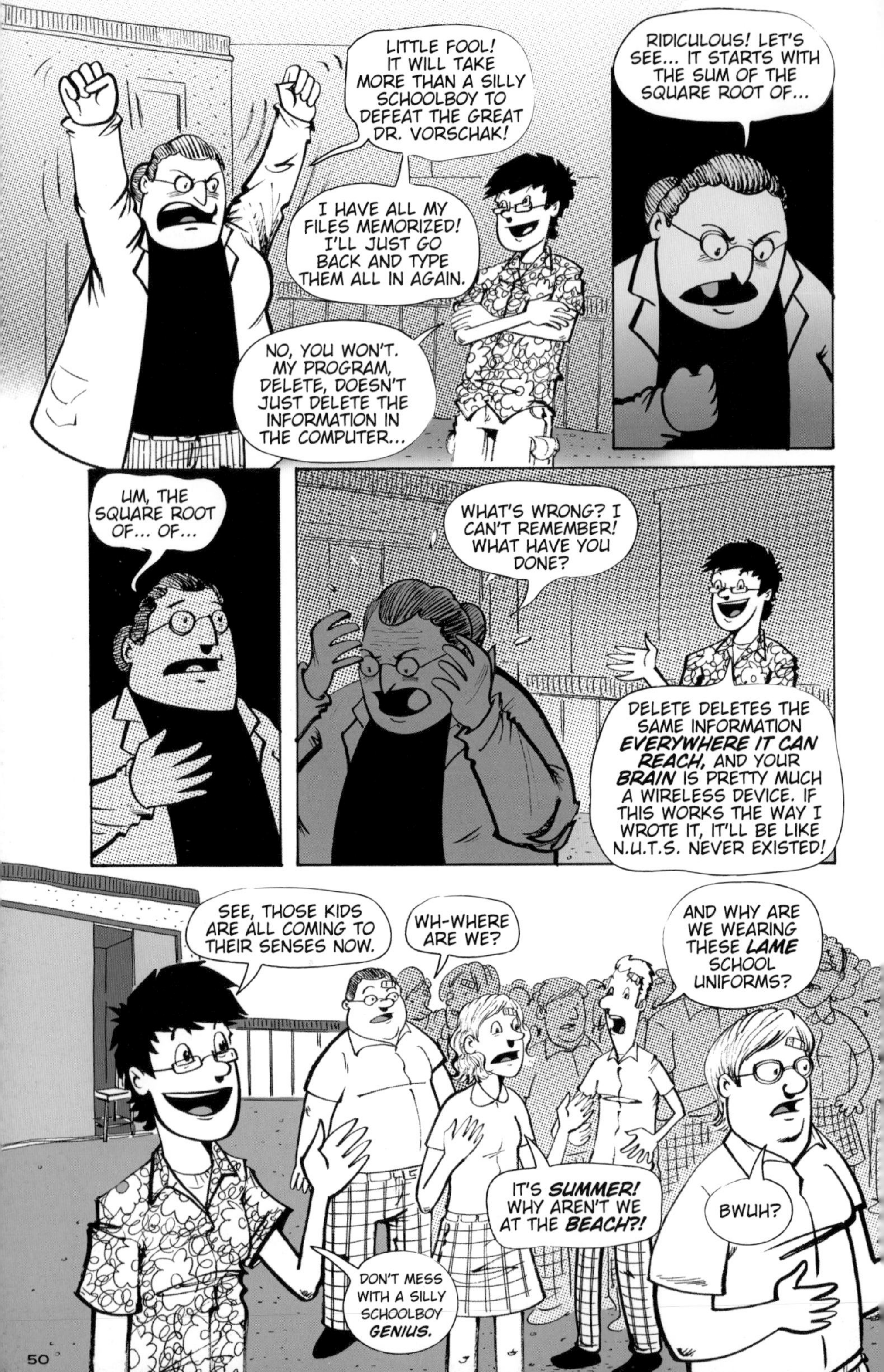
LITTLE FOOL! IT WILL TAKE MORE THAN A SILLY SCHOOLBOY TO DEFEAT THE GREAT DR. VORSCHAK!
I HAVE ALL MY FILES MEMORIZED! I'LL JUST GO BACK AND TYPE THEM ALL IN AGAIN.
NO, YOU WON'T. MY PROGRAM, DELETE, DOESN'T JUST DELETE THE INFORMATION IN THE COMPUTER...
RIDICULOUS! LET'S SEE... IT STARTS WITH THE SUM OF THE SQUARE ROOT OF...
UM, THE SQUARE ROOT OF... OF...
WHAT'S WRONG? I CAN'T REMEMBER! WHAT HAVE YOU DONE?
DELETE DELETES THE SAME INFORMATION ***EVERYWHERE IT CAN REACH,*** AND YOUR ***BRAIN*** IS PRETTY MUCH A WIRELESS DEVICE. IF THIS WORKS THE WAY I WROTE IT, IT'LL BE LIKE N.U.T.S. NEVER EXISTED!
SEE, THOSE KIDS ARE ALL COMING TO THEIR SENSES NOW.
WH-WHERE ARE WE?
AND WHY ARE WE WEARING THESE ***LAME*** SCHOOL UNIFORMS?
IT'S ***SUMMER!*** WHY AREN'T WE AT THE ***BEACH?!***
BWUH?
DON'T MESS WITH A SILLY SCHOOLBOY ***GENIUS.***

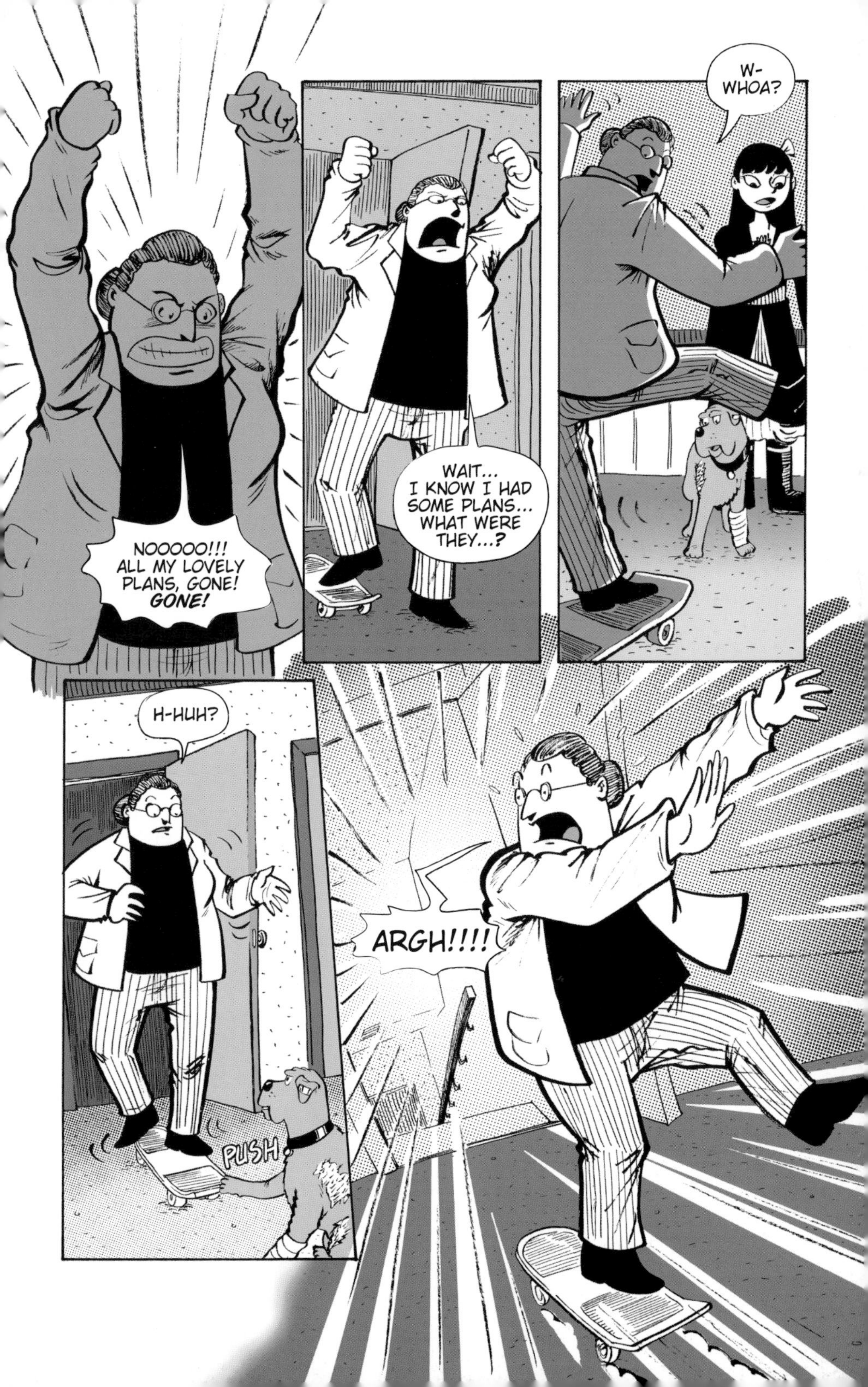
NOOOOO!!!
ALL MY LOVELY
PLANS, GONE!
GONE!
WAIT...
I KNOW I HAD
SOME PLANS...
WHAT WERE
THEY...?
W-
WHOA?
H-HUH?
PUSH
ARGH!!!!

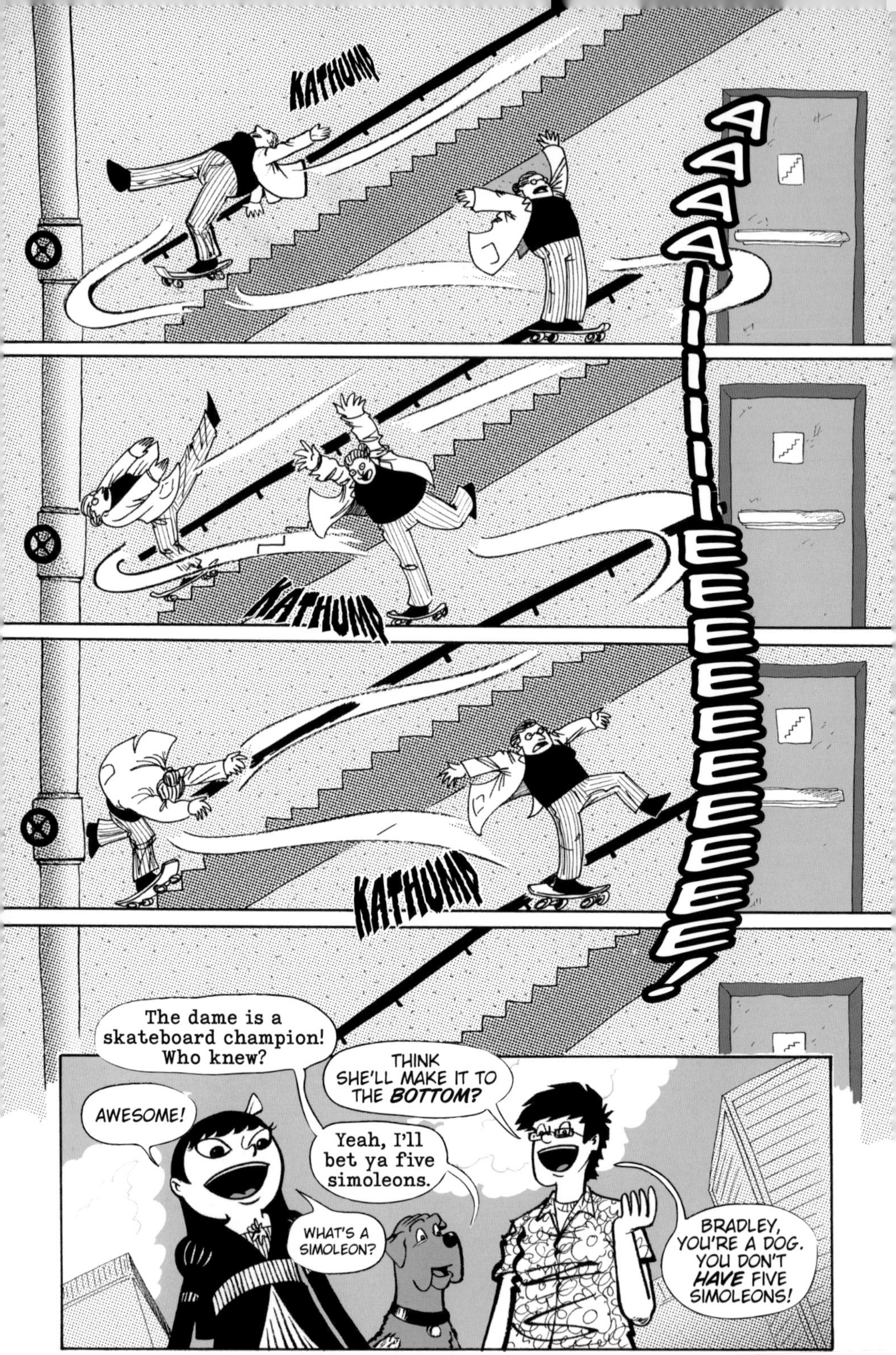
KATHUMP
AAAAIIIIIIEEEEEEEEEEE!
KATHUMP
KATHUMP
The dame is a skateboard champion! Who knew?
AWESOME!
THINK SHE'LL MAKE IT TO THE *BOTTOM?*
Yeah, I'll bet ya five simoleons.
WHAT'S A SIMOLEON?
BRADLEY, YOU'RE A DOG. YOU DON'T *HAVE* FIVE SIMOLEONS!

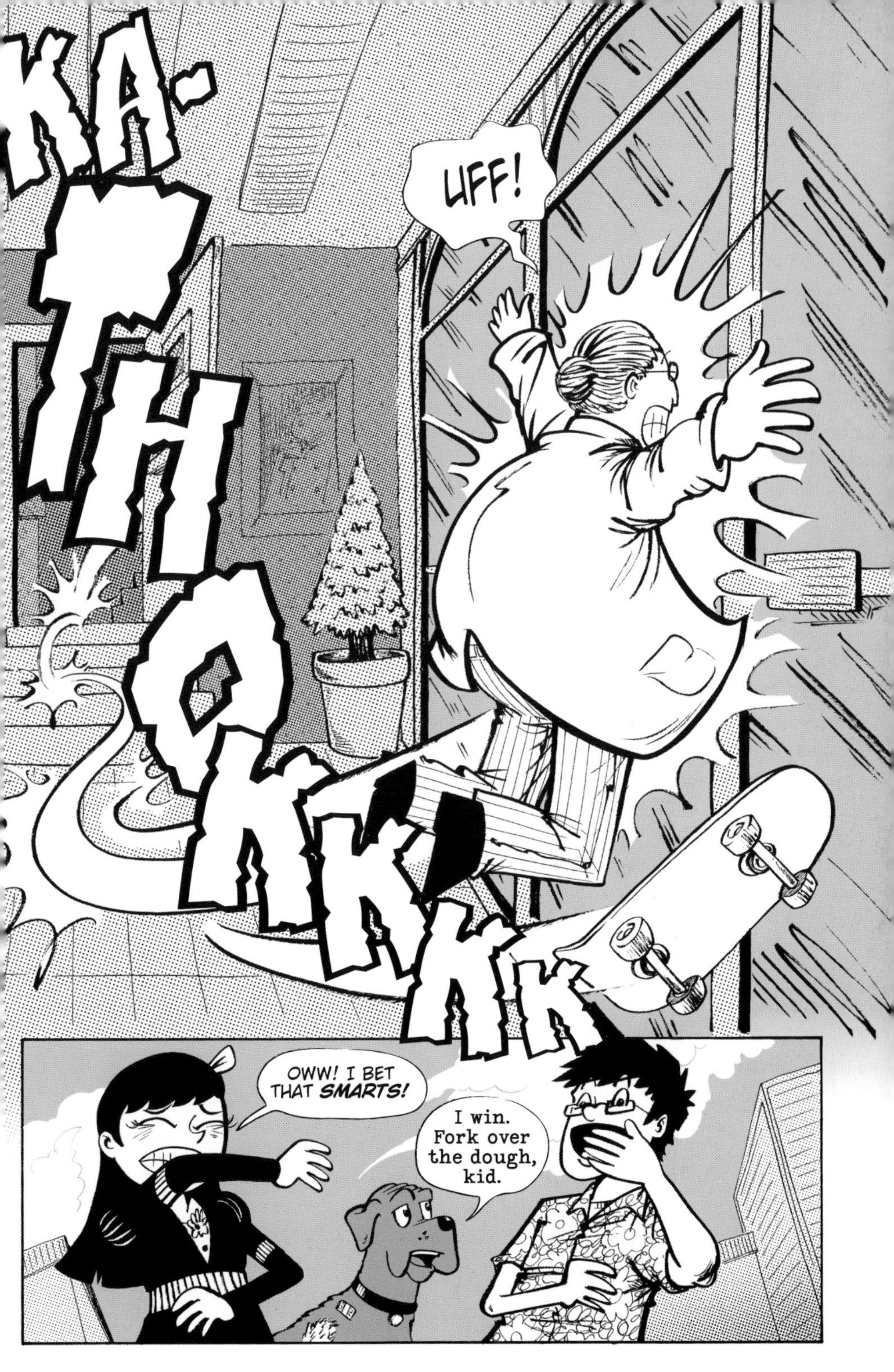

KA-THOKKKK
UFF!
OWW! I BET THAT SMARTS!
I win. Fork over the dough, kid.

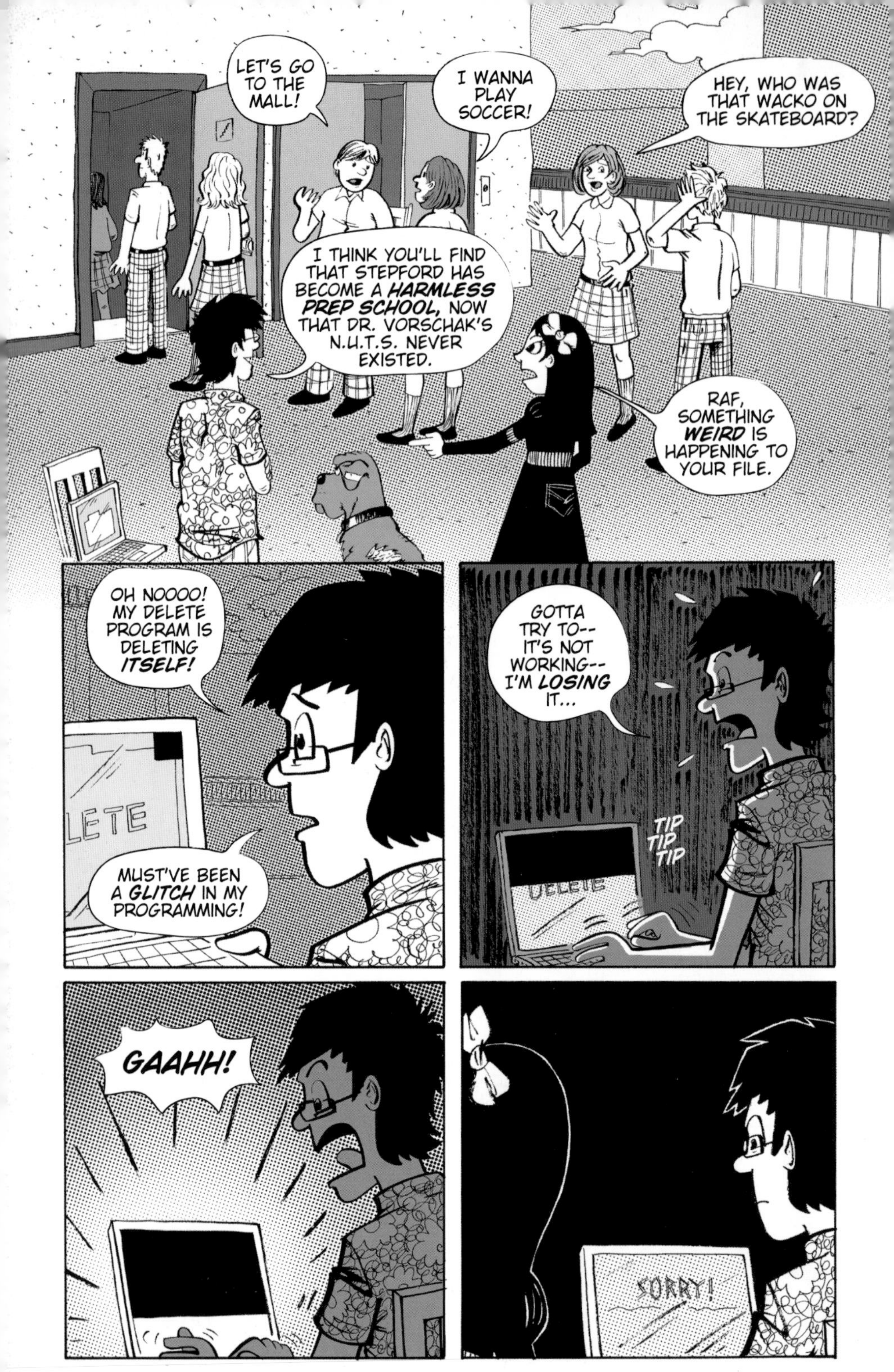
LET'S GO TO THE MALL!
I WANNA PLAY SOCCER!
HEY, WHO WAS THAT WACKO ON THE SKATEBOARD?
I THINK YOU'LL FIND THAT STEPFORD HAS BECOME A HARMLESS PREP SCHOOL, NOW THAT DR. VORSCHAK'S N.U.T.S. NEVER EXISTED.
RAF, SOMETHING WEIRD IS HAPPENING TO YOUR FILE.
OH NOOOO! MY DELETE PROGRAM IS DELETING ITSELF!
LETE
MUST'VE BEEN A GLITCH IN MY PROGRAMMING!
GOTTA TRY TO-- IT'S NOT WORKING-- I'M LOSING IT...
TIP TIP TIP
DELETE
GAAHH!
SORRY!

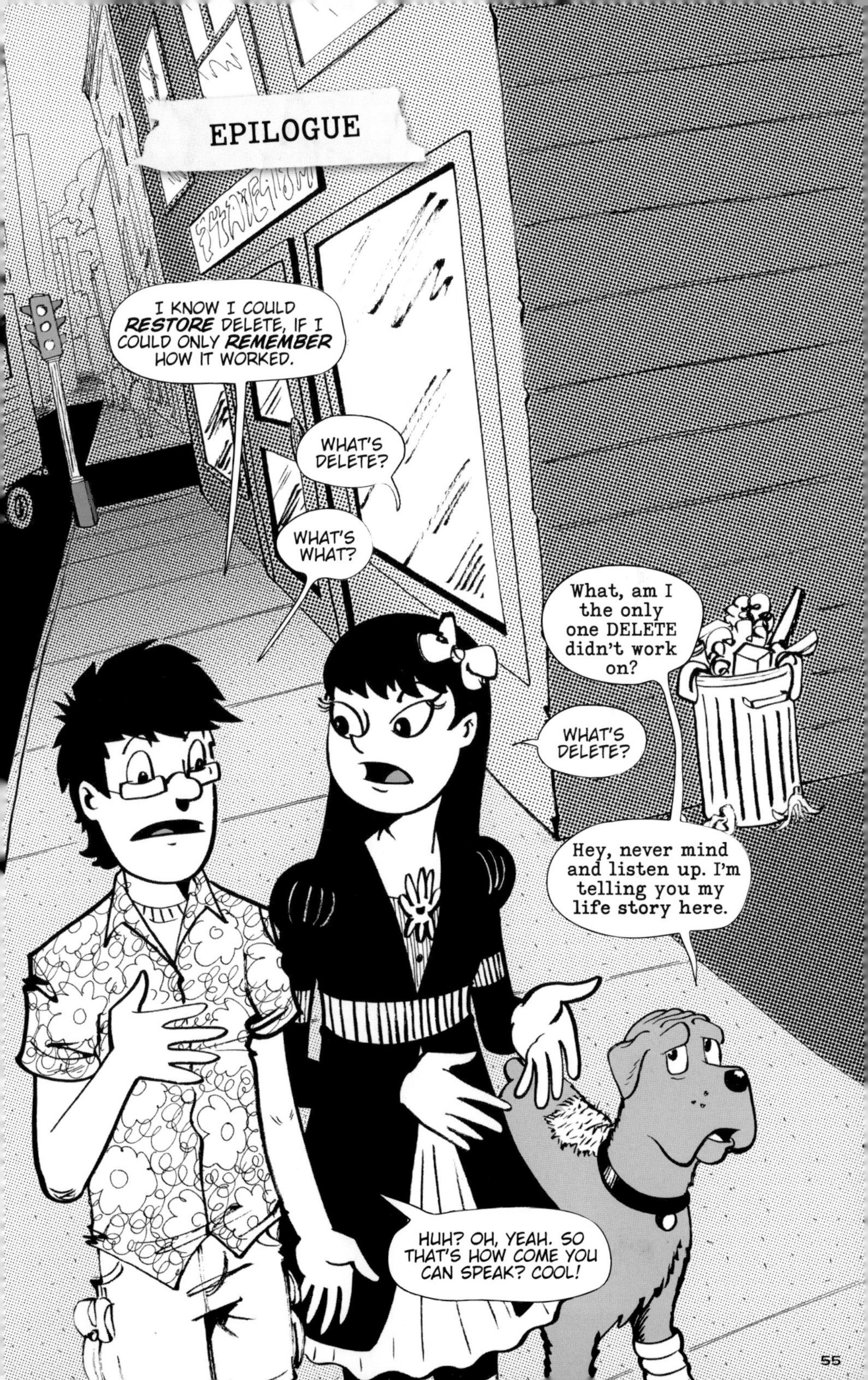
EPILOGUE
I KNOW I COULD RESTORE DELETE, IF I COULD ONLY REMEMBER HOW IT WORKED.
WHAT'S DELETE?
WHAT'S WHAT?
What, am I the only one DELETE didn't work on?
WHAT'S DELETE?
Hey, never mind and listen up. I'm telling you my life story here.
HUH? OH, YEAH. SO THAT'S HOW COME YOU CAN SPEAK? COOL!

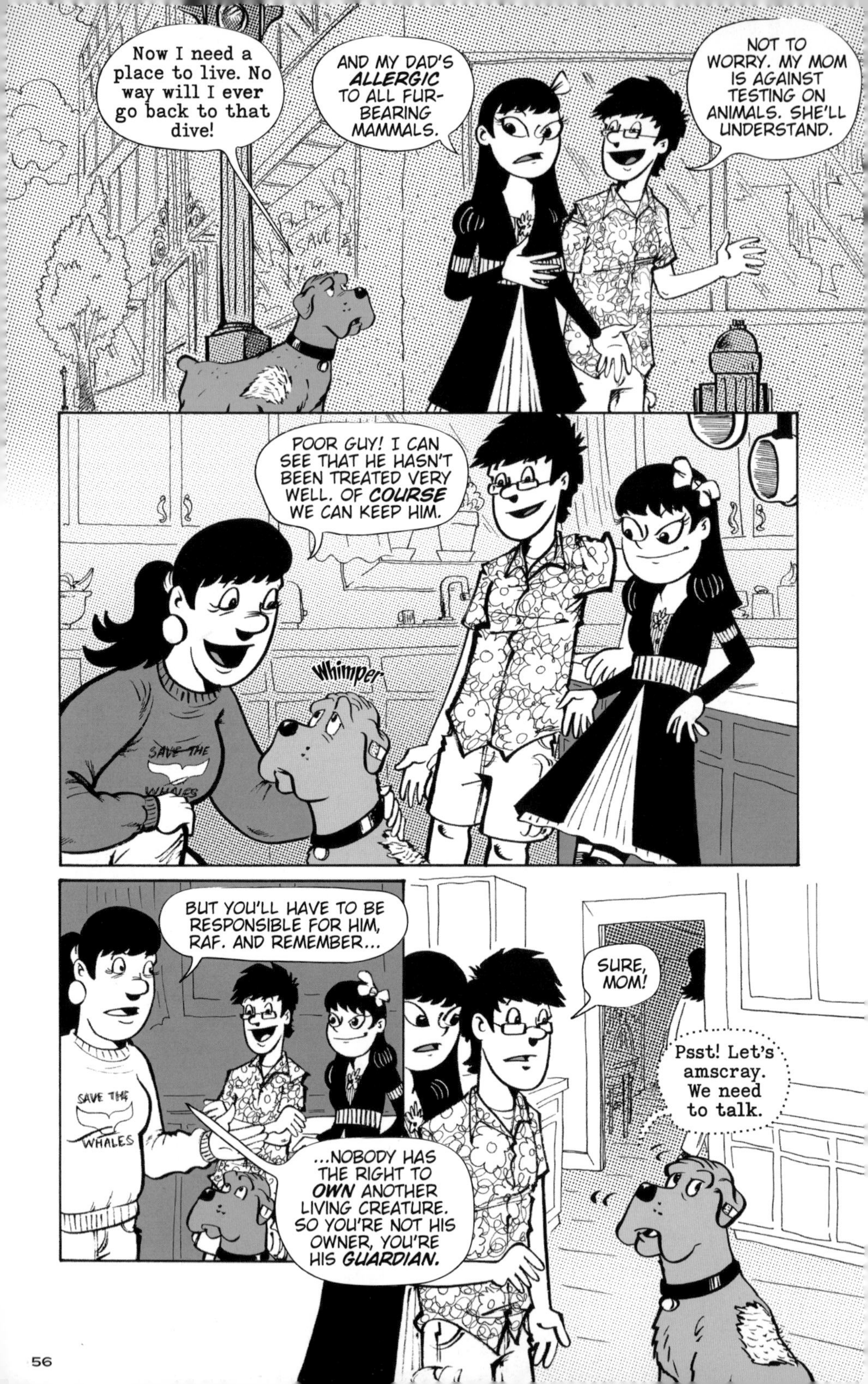
Now I need a place to live. No way will I ever go back to that dive!
AND MY DAD'S **ALLERGIC** TO ALL FUR-BEARING MAMMALS.
NOT TO WORRY. MY MOM IS AGAINST TESTING ON ANIMALS. SHE'LL UNDERSTAND.
POOR GUY! I CAN SEE THAT HE HASN'T BEEN TREATED VERY WELL. OF **COURSE** WE CAN KEEP HIM.
SAVE THE
Whimper
BUT YOU'LL HAVE TO BE RESPONSIBLE FOR HIM, RAF. AND REMEMBER...
SAVE THE WHALES
...NOBODY HAS THE RIGHT TO **OWN** ANOTHER LIVING CREATURE. SO YOU'RE NOT HIS OWNER, YOU'RE HIS **GUARDIAN.**
SURE, MOM!
Psst! Let's amscray. We need to talk.

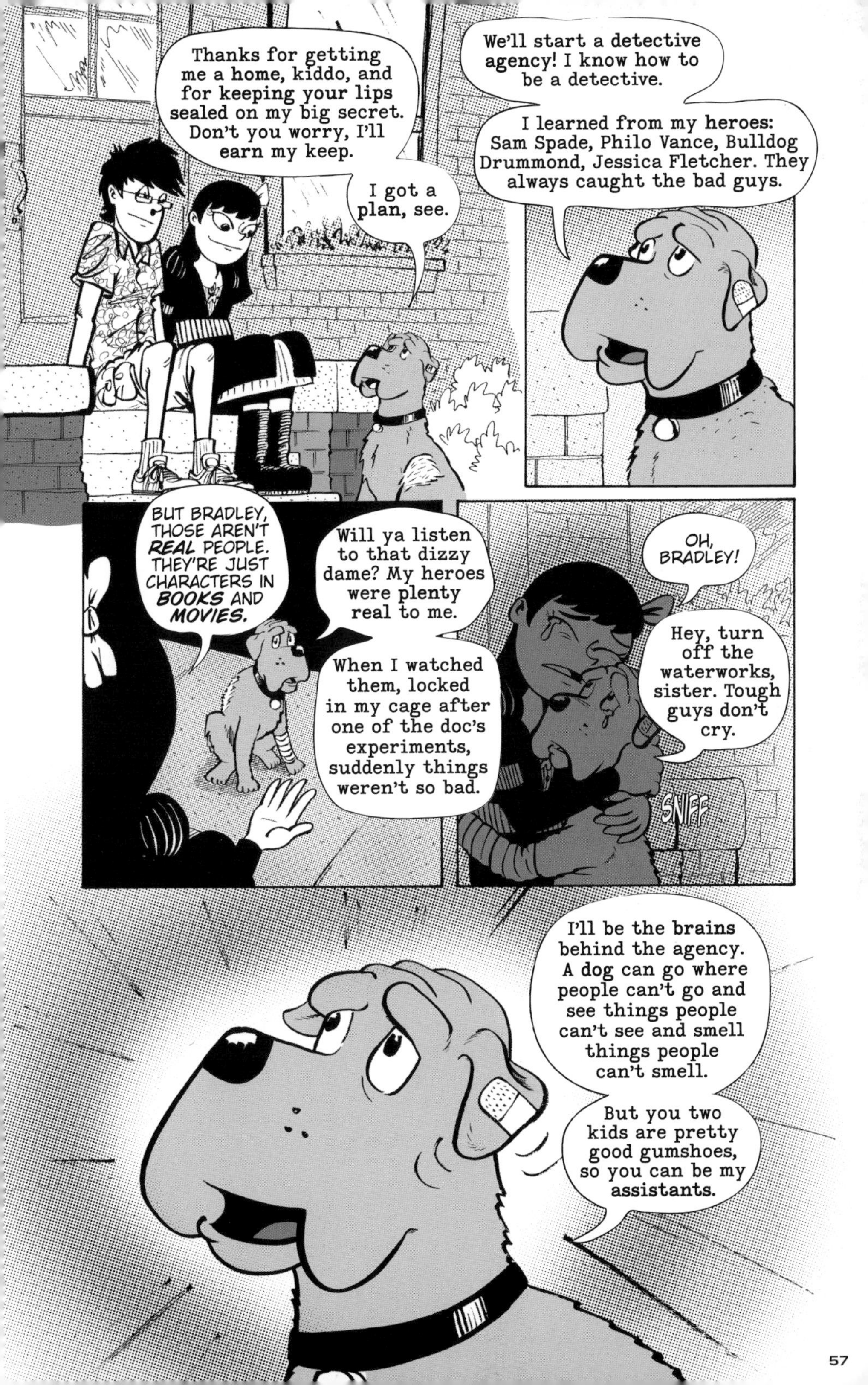
Thanks for getting me a home, kiddo, and for keeping your lips sealed on my big secret. Don't you worry, I'll earn my keep.
I got a plan, see.
We'll start a detective agency! I know how to be a detective.
I learned from my heroes: Sam Spade, Philo Vance, Bulldog Drummond, Jessica Fletcher. They always caught the bad guys.
BUT BRADLEY, THOSE AREN'T REAL PEOPLE. THEY'RE JUST CHARACTERS IN BOOKS AND MOVIES.
Will ya listen to that dizzy dame? My heroes were plenty real to me.
When I watched them, locked in my cage after one of the doc's experiments, suddenly things weren't so bad.
OH, BRADLEY!
Hey, turn off the waterworks, sister. Tough guys don't cry.
SNIFF
I'll be the brains behind the agency. A dog can go where people can't go and see things people can't see and smell things people can't smell.
But you two kids are pretty good gumshoes, so you can be my assistants.

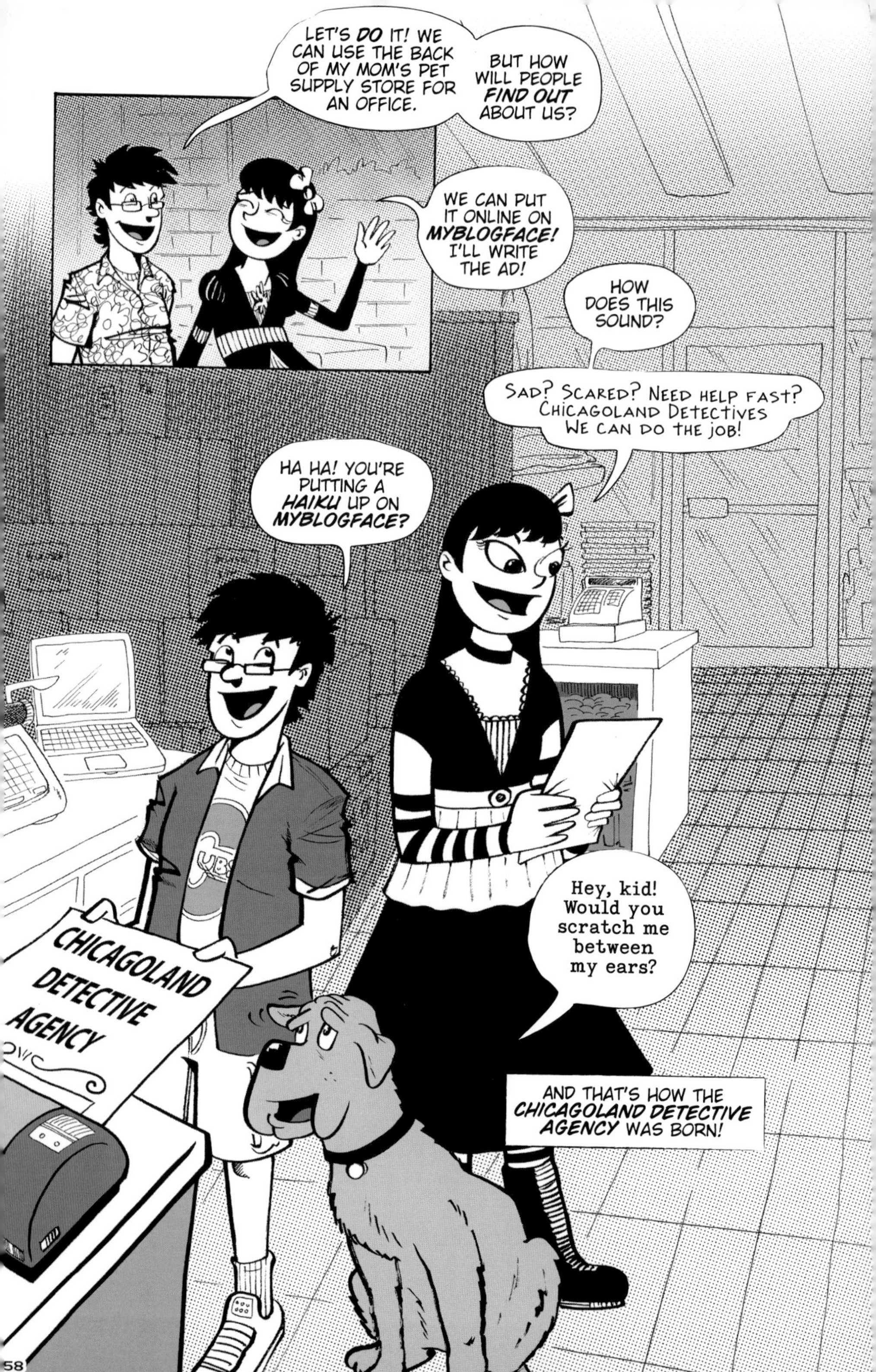
LET'S DO IT! WE CAN USE THE BACK OF MY MOM'S PET SUPPLY STORE FOR AN OFFICE.
BUT HOW WILL PEOPLE FIND OUT ABOUT US?
WE CAN PUT IT ONLINE ON MYBLOGFACE! I'LL WRITE THE AD!
HOW DOES THIS SOUND?
Sad? Scared? Need help fast? Chicagoland Detectives We can do the job!
HA HA! YOU'RE PUTTING A HAIKU UP ON MYBLOGFACE?
CHICAGOLAND DETECTIVE AGENCY
Hey, kid! Would you scratch me between my ears?
AND THAT'S HOW THE CHICAGOLAND DETECTIVE AGENCY WAS BORN!

Login: chicagoland

Password: •••••••n|

Click here to interFACE

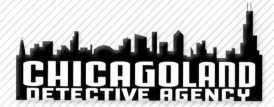

MYBLOGFACE

InforFACEtion

Location: Behind the counter of Hernandez & Sons Pet Supplies

Hours: 9–5 during summer vacation. During the rest of the year, afterschool hours, except on weekends

Proprietor: Raf Hernandez (that's me) because it's my mom's store

Friendly FACErs

3 Friends

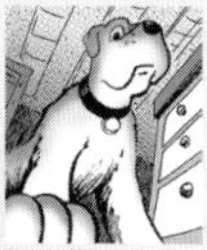

Bradley

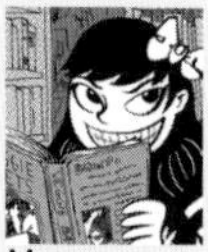

Megan Yamamura

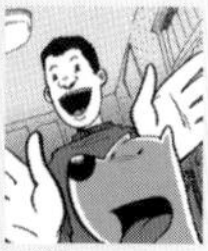

William Johnson

Meet the FACE

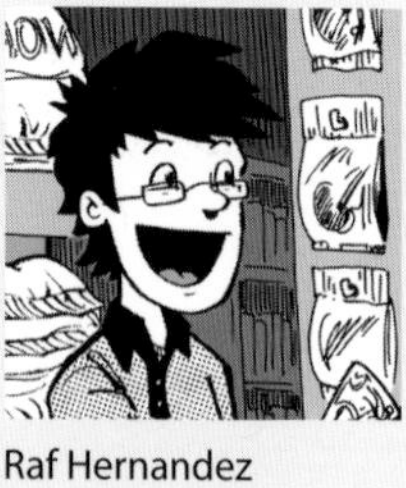

Raf Hernandez

Age: 12

Education: James A. Garfield Middle School

CHICAGOLAND DETECTIVE AGENCY

Our motto:

Sad? Scared? Need help fast?

Chicagoland Detectives:

We can do the job!

The Chicagoland Detective Agency is here for you. We solve low crimes and misdemeanors, and we battle injustice. Don't be afraid to come in with your pets. We love animals.

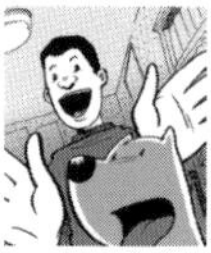

William Hey, dude, thanks for helping me keep my dog. The Chicagoland Detective Agency rules!

July 18 at 1:15 PM

Raf Hernandez's Bio

Favorite quote:
Wherever you are, there you are.

About Me:
When I was five years old, my mom discovered that I was writing math problems on her computer, so she bought me one of my own. I guess that makes me a computer geek. But it also makes me qualified to solve crimes the twenty-first century way: by using computer technology while my assistant, Megan Yamamura, does the legwork.

Ice cream: Chocolate or vanilla?
Rocky road.

Food: Hamburger or fried chicken?
Fried chicken, but my mom won't let me have it unless it's free-range. That means that instead of being stuck in tiny, cramped boxes where they can't even move, the chickens get to run around and peck at stuff on the ground.

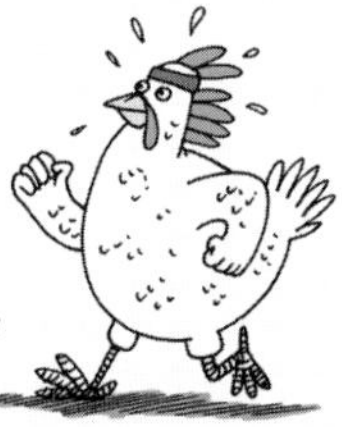

MYBLOGFACE

Meet the FACE

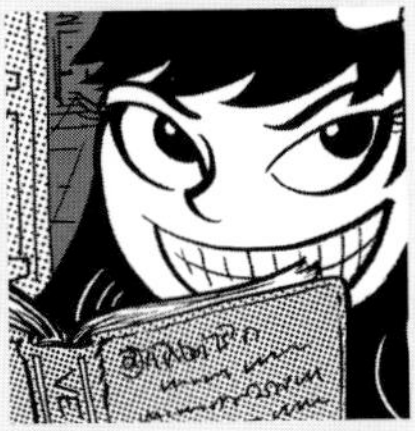

Megan Yamamura
Age: 13
Education: Stepford Preparatory Academy
Profession: Detective

Friendly FACErs

3 Friends

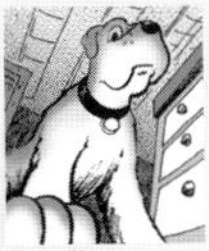

Bradley

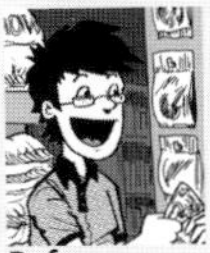

Raf Hernandez

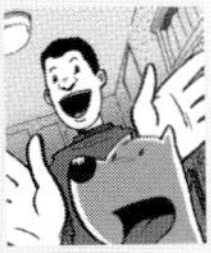

William Johnson

Megan Yamamura's Bio

Favorite quote:
An old pond
A frog jumping in—
The water's splash
(How cool is that? It's the most famous haiku in the world,
by the great Japanese poet, Basho.)

About Me:
I'm a poet, and my fave poetry is haiku, so that's what I write. Haiku is a form of Japanese poetry in three lines. In Japanese (even though not always in translation—see above!), the first and last lines have five syllables and the middle line has seven syllables, so that's how I write mine. You're probably thinking, pretty easy, I can do that. But actually haiku is supposed to paint a picture with words, to create a mood or feeling in just seventeen syllables, and that's not as easy as you think. Like that poem about the frog: can't you imagine sitting by that pond, and it's really quiet, and then—plop!

The haiku I write are not quite there yet, but I'm working on it.

The greatest haiku poet ever was Basho, who lived almost 400 years ago. He was born into a rich family, but he gave it all up to lead a simple life, wandering around the countryside, writing poetry. I want to live like that, but my father insists that I have to go to college and study medicine. We'll see!

I might change my mind, though, and become a manga-ka instead. That's someone who draws manga. My manga series, which will take fifty issues to complete, will be about a girl who gives up her medical career to lead a simple life, wandering around the countryside, writing poetry. And fighting ninjas.

But right now, before I become a manga-ka or a wandering poet, I'm being a detective. I never dreamed about being a detective before, but it's kind of fun. Before we even started the agency, Bradley says we had already foiled a mad scientist who was turning a whole school full of kids into zombies. Who knows what we'll do in the future? Anyway, I like my partners. Raf is really smart, even if he is a year younger than me, and Bradley is not only smart, he's soft and cuddly and cute. (But I never tell him that, because I know it would embarrass him.)

Ice cream: Chocolate or vanilla?
Soy ice cream, any flavor.

Food: Hamburger or fried chicken?
That's gross! I'm a vegetarian, and I won't eat anything that has a face. Soy is awesome!

Best friends:
Raf Hernandez and Bradley

CHICAGOLAND DETECTIVE AGENCY

Name: Bradley

Age: 2

Education: The school of hard knocks

Favorite quote: If you want me, just whistle.

Favorite book: THE KENNEL MURDER CASE, by S. S. Van Dine

Favorite movie: THE KENNEL MURDER CASE. (It was a book first, and then they made it into a movie, a long time ago. The hero, Philo Vance, has a dog and is a detective. On top of being a good detective, he loves his dog, so that's why Philo Vance is my favorite detective.)

Ice cream: Chocolate or vanilla? Gotta be vanilla, in small amounts. Dogs can't eat chocolate--AT ALL. It could kill us!

Food: Hamburger or fried chicken? Hamburger, raw please. Dogs can't eat chicken, either, because the bones could choke us or damage our stomachs. So, pal, if you love your dogs (and I hope you do!), lay off the chocolate and cooked chicken!

Best friends: Raf Hernandez and Megan Yamamura

I never knew my old man, and I can't remember my mom. And if that ain't enough, I spent two years as a captive of a loony dame named Dr. Vorschak. Her fiendish experiments on me turned me into a doggy Einstein. But now I have finally found a family with Raf and Megan. Of course, the world has to think that Raf is the big boss of our detective agency. Only Raf and Megan know that I'm the real brains behind the outfit.

Megan and Raf are swell kids, but they can't be more than sidekicks. Their little tiny noses aren't any good for tracking people by their smell. Dogs can smell fear!

I learned how to be a gumshoe from my heroes, like Philo Vance and Sam Spade. Megan says all those private eyes I watched on Dr. Vorschak's TV aren't real, just made-up characters in books and movies, but to me, they're as real as the slipper I chewed on this morning.

From those old detective movies, I learned that my heroes had a strong sense of justice. They couldn't rest until they solved the crimes and caught the bad guys, and I thought, us dogs are like that. Once we get our teeth into something, we don't wanna let go. A dog's gotta do what a dog's gotta do, so we make good detectives.

We may be small, but we have big hearts!